ROOTING
>>> FOR <<<
RAFAEL
ROSALES

KURTIS SCALETTA

Albert Whitman & Company
Chicago, Illinois

For Beverly Cleary, who showed that the
inner lives of children could be the whole story

Library of Congress Cataloging-in-Publication
data is on file with the publisher.

Text copyright © 2017 by Kurtis Scaletta
Published in 2017 by Albert Whitman & Company
ISBN 978-0-8075-6742-5
Printed in the United States of America
10 9 8 7 6 5 4 3 2 1 LB 22 21 20 19 18 17

Cover art copyright © 2016 by Kelsey Garrity-Riley
Design by Ellen Kokontis

For more information about Albert Whitman & Company,
visit our website at www.albertwhitman.com.

CHAPTER 1

Rafael, Many Years Ago

Rafael Rosales saw his first baseball game when he was five. He sprinted up the bleacher steps of Tetelo Vargas Stadium, flapped his arms, and pretended to fly. For a few glorious moments, he ran along the bench at the very top, his footsteps clanging, but when Papa got to the top, he tugged on Rafael's arm.

"Sit down or we'll leave now!" he threatened. Rafael plopped down on the bleacher. He could imagine Papa making them march out of the stadium before the game even started. His father wasn't a baseball fan and almost never spent money on fun things. He must have gotten the tickets for free.

Mama reached their seats carrying Iván, who was still a toddler. She handed Rafael a piece of candy to chew on. He leaned back and kicked up his feet and laughed. Papa settled him down with a firm hand. The stadium gradually filled up with people, most of them wearing the bright green of Las Estrellas Orientales. Rafael wished he had a cap with a shooting star like many of the fans wore. He wanted to feel like one of the crowd. He had never been a part of something so grand.

The fans roared and shook noisemakers as the Estrellas took to the field. The sound was deafening and wonderful. Children ran down to the front row and hung over the infield fence. Beautiful women in green skirts danced on top of the dugouts. Everybody stood still for the national anthem: "Valiant Quisqueyanos, let's raise our song!" At the end of the song, a merengue band started up. A man with the head of an elephant capered down on the field. Rafael started to dance, like many other fans, but Papa nudged him back into his seat.

At last, the game began, and Rafael stopped fidgeting and watched. He was fascinated at the ball whizzing by, fast as light, and the batter taking a swing. He was so excited to see the batter hit the ball that he hollered "Ayiiiiii!" as the ball sailed over the fence. A few fans gave him stern looks, but others laughed.

"The wrong team scored," Papa whispered sharply.

After that, Rafael watched the crowd. He cheered

when they cheered and groaned when they groaned. Mostly he watched the field, entranced. He finally understood why older boys in the barrio pretended to rear up and pitch oranges before peeling them, why they took practice swings with sticks they found in the street. They were imitating these men. He also wanted to run across green grass and hook a gleaming white ball out of the air while people whistled and clapped. He wanted to hit the ball and run in a circle and clap hands with the other players as he crossed the plate. He wanted to wave his cap at thousands of cheering people. He knew the word *béisbol*, but for the first time he understood all the wonder and magic that word held.

He knew then and lived by it every day after: this is what I want to do.

* * *

When he was seven years old and able to get away from the house and Mama's watchful eyes, Rafael inched closer and closer to the games that were always being played at the dead end of the street where there was no traffic.

He asked for a chance to swing the stick and was shoved aside by a slightly older boy in a New York

Yankees cap. Rafael had to hang back and simply watch with the other *niñitos*.

Even so, he started to watch the games every chance he got. He found out the older boy's name was Juan Santos Garcia. He overheard that Juan's cap had been sent by his uncle, who used to play professional baseball in the United States. More than once, Rafael saw Juan point out the shiny sticker on the cap. "That means it's authentic," Juan would say. He used the English word *authentic*, his tongue hissing against his teeth in the middle of the word.

Rafael got a chance to play a few weeks later. It was early in the morning after a heavy rain, and only a few boys were out to play.

"Rafael, you can join my team!" Juan called to him.

"I can play?" Rafael asked, unsure he'd heard him right. He didn't know that Juan even knew his name.

"Yes. You be defender." In street baseball, there was only one all-purpose fielder other than the pitcher and catcher. Rafael saw that the boy at the plate was right-handed, so he stood where a shortstop would be. He remembered this boy was a weak hitter and moved up a few steps. Juan saw that Rafael knew what to do and gave him a thumbs-up sign. "You're OK!" he said, using another expression from the United States.

Rafael did not have a glove, but he didn't need one. The ball was made of white socks pulled tight over a stone. He caught the ball the first time it was hit his way. He dropped it the second time but still got it to Juan for an out. The last boy struck out.

Juan gave him the stick.

"*Abres*," he said. Rafael knew the word to mean *open*, like a door. He hadn't heard it used in baseball.

"You mean I'm up first?"

"Yes. Try to get on base, and I will bring you home."

Rafael couldn't believe it. He was finally getting a chance to bat! He imitated every tough boy he had ever seen—tapping the plate with the stick and scowling at the pitcher. It was not really a plate, but a house-shape drawn in chalk.

The ball came at him, faster and closer than he'd thought it would. He swung at it, the way he had in all of his dreams, and made contact. The ball arced back to the pitcher, who caught it barehanded before Rafael could take a step. All of the boys cheered—he thought because he was out until Juan patted him on the shoulder.

"You almost got a hit!" he said. "You hit it hard! You're going to be a real *pelotero*."

CHAPTER 2

After that game, Rafael never had to wait long to play. And once he was in a game, he wouldn't quit until all the other boys had gone home or his mother dragged him home by his shirt collar. By his eighth birthday, he figured he was second best, after Juan. But he wasn't even a close second. Juan could leap up and nab a ball out of the air. Juan seemed to get a hit every time he batted.

One afternoon, a boy named Tomás hit a pop fly higher than any of them had ever seen. The boys stood and watched in awe as the ball hung in the air for a full countable second, spinning, before dropping back down.

"I bet I can hit it higher!" a boy named Diego shouted.

"No way, but I can!" The boys grappled for the makeshift bat. Rafael watched while they took turns popping the ball straight up in the air.

"Come on!" said Rafael. "We're playing a game." Nobody seemed to hear. Diego wrenched the bat free and took a turn. Tomás pitched while Diego flailed with the stick, trying to hit the ball straight in the air.

"It's my turn!" Another boy grabbed the bat away.

Juan edged over to Rafael and touched the brim of his beaten-up Yankees cap to say hello.

"Are you going to have a go?" he asked.

"A pop fly is usually an out. Why practice it?"

"Because it's fun."

"I don't care," said Rafael.

"Do you know the score right now?"

"Five to two. Your team is ahead."

Juan smirked, but not because he was winning. "Nobody else keeps score. You're so serious, Rafael. You have *fiebre*."

"No, I don't," said Rafael. His face flushed. Is this what the other boys thought of him? That he took himself too seriously?

"Yes, you do. It's all right."

"Hey, Yankee Juan!" Tomás called. "Do you want to try?"

"Sure!" Juan called back. "I'll show you how to hit a high one."

"Ooh, *Matatán* is going to show us!" Diego said.

"I'll show you all right." Juan strutted over and grabbed the stick from Diego. "I'll show you how to punch a hole in a cloud. I hope I don't hit an angel in the foot." The other boys laughed at Juan's patter.

"Let's let the big boss demonstrate!" Tomás reared back and threw a fast pitch instead of the underhanded lobs he'd been tossing to the others. Juan was ready for it. He swung and connected. The ball sailed up into the air, not as high as Tomás's, but higher than the tops of the houses.

"The big boss showed us!" Tomás said, his voice full of awe.

"Do it again," the other boys begged.

"Nah, let's play baseball," said Juan. He nodded slightly in Rafael's direction. "A pop fly is usually an out. Why practice it?"

"He knows he got lucky," Diego teased, but he walked out to his fielding position.

Rafael felt a pang of jealousy, not for the fly ball, but for the way the other boys did whatever Juan said.

* * *

For the next few weeks, Rafael played with new ferocity. He was out early every morning to practice before school. When nobody else showed up, he practiced throwing his own handmade ball hard against the sidewall of the *colmado* until the shopkeeper ordered him to stop. When he did play, he tried to knock the stone out of the socks every time he came to the plate. He scraped his knees and elbows chasing ground balls. If he was going to be known for his fever, he wanted his reputation to spread through the streets and reach the campo where the older boys played.

But as his fever grew, so did his impatience with the other boys. He ground his teeth when they got to chatting and didn't resume play. He fumed when they let easy grounders get by them. He never said a word, but he sensed the other boys didn't like him. They didn't joke with him as they did with each other.

One day, Tomás ducked out of the way when a hard-hit ball flew at his head.

"Don't act like a turtle," Rafael shouted, his frustration finally getting the better of him. "This ball is like a sponge! It won't hurt to hit you!" He threw it hard against his own forehead to demonstrate.

The other boys laughed so hard they nearly fell to the ground.

"You should listen to Rafael," said Juan. "He's the real deal." It was another *estadounidense* expression he'd picked up. None of the boys knew what it meant, but they knew Juan was scolding them. The laughter died down.

"*Lo siento*," Tomás muttered.

Later the same day, Diego attempted a new pitch— he called it "the blind man's curve" and threw with his eyes closed, missing the batter by a mile. Rafael had seen entire games fall apart when that kind of nonsense got started.

"Pitch normal," he said.

"Sorry," Diego said, and threw an eyes-open pitch.

* * *

After the game, Juan surprised Rafael by stepping up behind him and throwing an arm around his shoulders.

"You should come to my house," he said.

"I should?" He had known Juan for a year and had never been invited to his house. He had not been invited to *anyone's* house.

"You need to meet my brother, Hugo. He's got the fever like you, pelotero." Juan led Rafael down the street, past rows of small concrete houses with tin roofs. Most of the houses were painted in bright colors, but some had been painted more recently than others.

"My papa will be there too. He's between jobs. Don't worry, he'll find work soon. He's one of the best at what he does."

"What's that?"

"He lays tiles. He helped build half the hotels between Boca Chica and Punta Cana. Helped make the floors, anyway." Juan stopped and tugged on Rafael's arm. "Have you ever been in La Playa de Mar Verde?"

"No." Mar Verde was where rich tourists stayed. Why would he have been inside?

"My papa tiled all the bathrooms on the first floor."

"*De verdad?*" Rafael thought Juan wanted him to be impressed, but the older boy snorted laughter and started walking again.

"Hugo is the best player in the barrio, Rafael. He's going to be a big star. He can throw a cutter like Rogério Romero. He's going to be a superstar, and then Papa won't have to crawl around in other people's bathrooms."

They reached a row of homes that had once been painted pink and yellow, but had flaked and paled in the sun and salty air. Juan led him through a door that was propped open with a brick. Rafael's stomach was tight with nervousness. He was excited to be friends with Juan, but what if his big brother didn't like him? Inside, a man and a boy were sitting on a stiff couch, listening to the radio. The walls were covered with framed photographs and pictures, unlike the blank walls in Rafael's own house. The boy was eleven or twelve. He looked like Juan but did not have Juan's easygoing smile. His lips were tight and turned down at the corners.

"Papa, Hugo. This is Rafael," said Juan.

This was Hugo? Rafael had imagined someone nearly full grown. Hugo was only a few years older than he was.

"Shh," said his father. "Rogério is pitching to Sanchez."

"Rogério Romero?" Rafael asked in a whisper. Before either could answer, cheers erupted three thousand miles away. The radio switched to a commercial.

"*Sí*, it was Rogério Romero," Hugo said excitedly. "Los Astros loaded the bases with no outs, but LA brought in Romero, and he struck out the side!"

"He's still got it," said Juan's father. He lowered his voice. "At least some days he's still got it."

"Papa knew Rogério when they were boys," Juan said.

"He struck me out a few times," said his father.

"Never saw a kid who could throw that hard until this one came along." He thumped Hugo on the back.

"I can pitch," Hugo admitted, beaming. He stood up and flexed his arm, as if he were stretching before a game.

"That campo behind the taxi stand, that's where Romero and my papa used to play," said Juan. His father offered a faint nod of agreement. "Hugo plays there now," said Juan. "And I'll play there soon."

"I know that field," said Rafael. You had to be good to get into those games, and older boys dominated.

"Rafael is a good player too," said Juan. "He never quits or goofs off. He's the most intense of anyone. He has the fever, like you. I wanted him to meet you."

"Sí?" Hugo looked at Rafael, appraised him, and cracked a wide grin. "If you're serious about ball, then why do you hang around with my goofy brother?" Juan playfully punched at Hugo, nearly knocking him back to the couch, but Hugo snared his hand and the two boys wrestled for a moment. Rafael backed up, bumping into a table that filled up the room.

"Oh, oh. Enough." Their father reached in and nudged Juan away. "Watch your hands."

"I'm fine," said Hugo. He held up his right hand

to the light shining through the paneless window and splayed his fingers. His hand was large for his body; silhouetted he looked like a child wearing a man's glove. "Hey, I'm pitching tomorrow. You should come see us play, *hermanito*. You too!" He nodded at Rafael.

Juan was looking at his own fingers, which were normal sized and looked like stumps compared to Hugo's. He dropped his hand. "Only if I can play."

"Ha. You wish, Mister Yankee." He took the brim of Juan's cap and yanked it down. "This hat barely fits you anymore, hermanito."

Juan straightened his cap. "It's all I got. And I would rather play in the street than see your game. I'm a player, not a spectator."

"You can play in a year or two," said Hugo.

"I'll come to your game," Rafael blurted out. At that moment, he would have followed Hugo into the Caribbean Sea if he'd suggested it.

CHAPTER 3

Rafael was too excited for the game after school to pay attention to his teacher. He would probably not be allowed to play, but he fantasized that he would be mistaken for older and put into the game.

"Rafael?" He sat up straight when he heard Señora Pereña say his name. What had she been talking about? What subject was it? "Can you tell us why Bartolomé Colón is important in our history?" she asked. Rafael's mind raced. He had heard of Bartolo Colon. Bartolomé must be his full name.

"He just won the Cy Young Award?"

"Good guess, but Bartolomé Colón founded Santo Domingo in 1498. You have heard of Cristobál, his brother?" The class burst into laughter. Cristobál Colón was the most famous person in history, probably. He brought Jesus and Spanish to the Americas. There were cities and countries named for him, statues and a giant lighthouse in Santo Domingo. Rafael wanted to disappear. What was the point of school, anyway? It was all multiplication tables and indirect objects and white men on boats. None of it would do him any good when he played baseball.

The day dragged on even slower than usual. He watched the clock, as he often did, counting the tick marks toward the end of school. Fortunately, he did not get called on again.

He had to take Iván home before he could go to the baseball field to see Hugo play. Iván prattled about what he'd learned in kindergarten: a story about a stray cat who became king, a song about sunshine and rain.

"I like school," he said. "I like it a lot."

"Sure, it's all stories and songs in kindergarten. Wait until you have to learn about Bartolomé Colón."

They arrived at home.

Mama was waiting at the door, and Rafael nudged Iván toward her.

"See you later."

"Rafael, play with your brother," his mother said.

"I'm too busy to keep an eye on him today. Besides, he misses you."

"I can't!" said Rafael. "I have a game today!"

"You play ball every day. You can miss it once in awhile," she said.

Rafael saw Iván looking up at him with hopeful eyes.

"What if I take him with me?"

"No," she said. "Stay close to the house."

The unfairness of it was hard to take, but Rafael never argued with Mama. It would be like arguing with the sky when it rained: Mama decided how things would be, and that was that.

Rafael took his brother in the opposite direction of the streetball games; he did not want those boys to see them. He walked quickly, making Iván hurry to keep up.

"Mama said to stay close," Iván whined.

"We aren't that far!" said Rafael. But they were nearly to the busy Calle Mir, which he wasn't allowed to cross. There was a gap between a church and the row of houses where Juan and Hugo lived. "We can play here."

"Can we play pirates?"

"Sure," said Rafael, "whatever you want."

They lobbed pebble-sized cannonballs at an invisible ship in the distance and fought off the invaders with swords. After making them walk the plank, Rafael climbed a stout palm tree and pretended it was the mast of a ship. He made a telescope of his hand and searched the horizon. He looked in the direction of the game he was missing and saw a slump-shouldered boy crossing the Calle Mir. It was Hugo. Why was he leaving the game so early? It had not even been an hour since school got out.

Rafael dropped to the ground. "I saw an island that way! I think there's treasure!"

"We have to take a boat." His brother turned around and pretended to row. Rafael followed, walking backward and feeling foolish. Hugo was sitting on the curb in front of his house, his worn baseball glove resting on his knee.

"*Hola*, Rafael."

"Hola, Hugo." Rafael stopped. Iván stopped too and looked curiously at Hugo. "I thought you were pitching today," said Rafael.

Hugo stared at his glove, then looked up and grinned. "I got lit up like the Faro a Colón."

"He what?" Iván looked up at Rafael. "He says he's a lighthouse?"

"He means he had a bad game," Rafael whispered. He could explain baseball slang later. "I wanted to watch, but I had to take care of my brother," he explained.

"We're pirates!" said Iván. "Give us all your gold!"

Hugo patted his pockets. "I have some doubloons right here." He pretended to give Iván some of the pesos and made clinking noises with his tongue as the imaginary coins changed hands.

"Thanks!" said Iván.

"What are you going to buy with all that?" Hugo asked.

"I'm going to buy a baseball glove for my brother and an elephant for me."

"You know, I saw an elephant for sale down there." He pointed Iván back toward home and winked at Rafael.

"Let's go!" Iván tugged on Rafael's hand. Rafael anchored his feet. He wanted to keep talking to Hugo. Iván sprang loose and took off down the street.

"I remember when Juan was that age," said Hugo. "He never wanted to do anything alone."

"Sí," Rafael agreed. "Iván is the same way." It wasn't true, but he liked the way Hugo was talking to him—eye to eye, big brother to big brother.

Hugo stood up. "Well, I better go in and tell Papa what happened." He slapped hands with Rafael. "You better chase your brother down and help him buy his elephant."

CHAPTER 4

Rafael wanted to be the kind of big brother that Hugo was to Juan. He wanted to tug the brim of his brother's cap down over his eyes. He wanted Iván to boast to friends that his big brother was a future star.

It also occurred to him that Iván was now six, almost the same age he'd been when he started watching the streetball games. He had been seven, but he hadn't had a big brother to take care of him.

"You should come with me tomorrow," he told Iván that night in bed.

"I don't like baseball," said Iván.

"How do you know? You've never played."

"I've seen enough to know I don't like it."

Rafael got up on one elbow to look his brother in the face. "Come on," he said. "I played pirates with you today. You can play baseball with me tomorrow."

"Maybe," said Iván. The next day he followed Rafael to the dead-end street where they played. Rafael saw that there were more boys than could play. "Go stand with the other little kids to watch," he told Iván.

"I thought I'd get to play!"

"Watch and learn the game first," said Rafael. "You'll get a chance."

"At least let me stay with you."

Rafael sighed. "I have my brother today," he announced. "He's not really playing, but he wants to stay with me."

"*Mamá gallina* Rafael brought his *polluelo*!" Tomás hooted.

"Why did he call you a mother hen and me a chick?" Iván wondered.

"He's still mad because I called him a turtle once."

"A turtle!" Iván shouted. "That's funny."

"Shh," Rafael whispered.

Iván stayed close to him until the game started, and when Rafael batted, Iván ran after him. Rafael reached base safely, but Tomás tagged Iván.

"Polluelo is out!"

"No I'm not! Leave me alone, you dumb *tortuga*."

Iván pushed past him and tried to join Rafael on the base.

"You're out," Tomás insisted. He pulled Iván away by the shoulder—a little roughly, Rafael thought.

"What are you doing? He's not even really playing." Rafael stepped off the base, and Tomás tagged him out as well.

"Double play!" he shouted. "That's the third out."

"Don't be a cheater."

"You're the one who wants extra players on your team."

"Oh, come on!" He looked to Juan for support. His friend looked grim. "Tomás is right," Juan decided. "That's two outs."

"Fine," said Rafael. He walked over to his fielding position. "You play there." He sent Iván several paces back and hoped he would stay out of the way.

Juan batted first and bounced the ball their way. Rafael scooped it up but found Iván between him and the base.

"Let me out him!" Iván begged, tugging on Rafael's arm. "I want to out him!"

"Not now!" Rafael couldn't get free. Juan touched the base and ran around to score.

"You shouldn't play when your polluelo needs you, gallina!" Juan hollered with a laugh. Gallina meant *hen*, but it could also mean a sissy and a coward. It was a fighting word in the barrio. Rafael didn't care when Tomás used it, but it hurt when Juan did.

"I'm no gallina!" he shouted.

"Take a joke," said Juan.

Rafael tried to slow his heart from racing. He turned to Iván.

"Stay out of my way, or go home," he snapped. Iván froze, tears welling up in his eyes. That made Rafael feel bad, so the next time he came to the plate, he gave the stick to Iván.

"Take my turn at the plate," he said. He nudged Iván toward the plate. "Nothing hard," he said to Juan. But before Juan could throw a single pitch, Iván was running straight at him, wielding the stick like a club. Juan turned to escape the blows, and Iván whapped him again and again in the backside.

"You don't call my brother a gallina! You're the gallina!" Iván shouted. Rafael caught him, picked him up, and hauled him away while he was still thrashing and screaming. Juan was curled up on the ground, his Yankees cap knocked askew.

Rafael had to tell Mama what happened, because Iván's eyes were red, his face streaked with dirt and tears. Mama told Papa when he got home. He sighed heavily, sat down at the table, and asked both boys to come over.

"Your mother says you boys were in a fight?"

"We're sorry." Rafael hung his head. He hadn't been part of the fight, but he knew better than to argue with his parents. Besides, he knew he was responsible for what his little brother did when they were together.

"I'm not sorry!" said Iván. "They called us names."

"You can't fight every time somebody calls you a name," said Papa.

"Yes I can!" Iván clenched both fists like he might take a swing at Papa, and to Rafael's surprise, Papa laughed.

"You are like me as a boy, *pugilista*." He reached out and pulled Iván to him, wrapping his arms around his shoulders. "But if you two keep fighting with those boys, you can't play with them anymore."

"That's not fair!" Rafael exclaimed, forgetting about not arguing with his father. "Iván was the one who started it!"

But as he said it, he realized it would not be easy to go back anyway, not after what had happened. How could he face Juan ever again? Juan was the one who'd invited him to play in the first place, and he seemed to be the only boy who liked Rafael.

That night Iván nudged Rafael. They were lying in bed, listening to the sounds of the city drifting through the window: loud voices and radios, car horns and music.

"I'm sorry I hit that boy," said Iván.

"*Lo que ha pasado pasado*," said Rafael. What happened, happened.

CHAPTER 5

Several weeks passed, and Rafael did not play. He waited for someone to come get him, to ask why he hadn't shown up for streetball, but nobody did. That made it harder to go back.

One Sunday, Papa took Rafael and Iván to the sugarcane farm where he worked. "We'll give your mother some time to herself," he explained, driving a battered truck he sometimes borrowed from work. The farm and factory were closed on Sundays, but Papa's work was never done. His mind was always on the machines. "In every corner, something is breaking," he would mutter over his coffee in the morning and his beans and rice at lunch. He worried about the machines the way the neighbors worried about the Estrellas, who were also always on the verge of breaking down.

Normally Rafael would find a bat-sized stalk to break and swing. This time he didn't. His baseball days were done. Instead he played *cache-cache* with Iván. They took turns hiding and finding each other among the high stalks. After a few rounds, Iván wanted to race.

"I can beat you!" he shouted, running and disappearing into the cane. Rafael ran after him, holding back to let Iván think he was winning, but sprinting ahead as they came to the edge of the field. He finished one pace ahead.

"I am first! I am the best!" he shouted.

Iván laughed, then stopped. He pointed at a cluster of shacks and shanties where the cane pickers lived, no more than a kilometer from the building where Papa worked.

"What's this?"

"It's the batey. You've seen it before."

But Iván must not have remembered.

"Do people live here?"

"Yes. They live here because they work here."

"Papa works here, and we don't live here," said Iván.

"Of course not," said Rafael. "Papa doesn't pick cane."

"I don't like it here," said Iván.

Rafael saw the batey for the first time with clear eyes—the leaky tin roofs of the shacks, the muddy lanes winding among the homes, the old boards that served for doors.

"It isn't great," he agreed. It wasn't simply that the people were poor. People were poor everywhere. These people seemed forgotten, like something left to spoil in the sun.

A girl, three or four years old, chased after a chicken that had gotten loose and was hopping and flapping between the shacks. Rafael saw where it was headed and blocked its route. He was able to get his hands around the tame bird. The bird was smaller than it looked—all fluff and feathers. He handed it to her, and she took it—firmly, but gently.

"*Mesi!*" she said. He'd traded a few words with the cane pickers before. Some were Haitian and spoke Creole. Others were Cocolo and spoke Caribbean English. This girl must be Haitian. He knew that "Mesi," was "thank you."

"*De nada,*" he replied, because he didn't know how to respond in Creole. "*Bonjou.*"

"What did you say to her?"

"I said hello. That's how they say hello."

"Bonhoo," Iván attempted. The girl grinned, showing a gap between her front teeth.

"*Mwen se Bij*," she said.

"What did she say that time?" Iván asked in Spanish.

"I don't know," Rafael admitted.

"Does she really live here? All the time?" Iván whispered.

"Don't be rude," Rafael whispered back. Most of the cane pickers knew a little Spanish, and Rafael didn't want anybody to hear Iván's questions. He waved good-bye to the girl and led Iván back into the sugarcane.

"Of course they live there all the time," he answered once they were out of earshot of the batey. "What did you think?"

"I thought they might have nicer houses somewhere."

"But they don't have any money," Rafael said, exasperated.

"Tell Papa to give them more money so they can build nicer houses."

"I will."

They found Papa inside the machine shed, tending to a machine with rows of curved blades.

"Why don't you pay the pickers enough to live better?" Rafael asked.

"Do you think that's my choice?" Papa asked. "Do you think I'm the boss of everything?"

Rafael gulped. He had thought that.

"Well, I'm not. I fix the machines and am boss of nobody. All of us are lucky to have jobs at all. Now let me work."

* * *

"What was that girl's name?" Iván asked Rafael that night in bed.

"How should I know?"

"You talked to her."

"She said thanks, and I said hello. That was it." There had been more, but he didn't understand it.

"Did she have lunch yesterday?"

"I'm sure she did."

"How do you know?"

"I don't. Stop asking questions." Rafael rolled over in bed to face the wall.

"Rafael." Iván nudged him again. Rafael turned back, ready to yell at Iván for annoying him, but the anger left him when he saw Iván's eyes were rimmed with tears.

"What?"

"Did that girl have to eat her pet chicken?"

Rafael bit the inside of his lip to keep himself from laughing.

"Well, did she?" Iván repeated.

"I don't know," said Iván. "Maybe. If she did, it wasn't a pet in the first place."

"Will you help her family when you're a famous baseball player with lots of money?"

"Sure," said Rafael. "If I become a famous baseball player."

How would that happen when he couldn't even play streetball? He could go back and beg Juan to let him play, but the thought made him sick to his stomach.

He closed his eyes and tried to imagine himself playing a real baseball game in a stadium with thousands of fans cheering his name. He used to imagine that every night before passing into sleep, but now he couldn't. Instead he saw the chicken fluttering down the muddy lane of the batey, the girl's smile as he handed her the bird.

A gallina, he thought bitterly. The bird was a gallina.

Getting called a name was a foolish thing to be angry about.

He would have to tell Juan he was sorry. Juan would say, "Sorry for what?" and laugh it off. "Where have you been?" he would ask. "We missed you." Or maybe Juan would scowl at him, tell him to *vete a la porra*.

Rafael opened his eyes. Iván was asleep now, though murmuring and fidgeting.

When morning came, Rafael wasn't sure he had slept at all. He dozed off during the teacher's lesson about Santo Domingo being seized by pirates—a true story, one he would have to tell Iván. He answered every question wrong on a math test and walked home.

He did not go to Juan or say he was sorry that day, or the next, or the next.

CHAPTER 6

Maya, This Year

Maya scanned the smattering of other early comers at the stadium: a mix of old people whiling away the day; families, like hers, on vacation; and men in groups of three or four, all of them in baseball caps and jerseys, some toting big plastic cups of beer even though it was barely 11:00 a.m.

She didn't see how anyone could care about baseball when the ice caps were melting and the bees were dying. She wished she were still at the hotel.

"Why do I have to go?" she'd asked. "I don't even like baseball."

"Because it's a family vacation," Mom told her.

"Then why isn't Dad coming?"

"Touché," Mom said. "You're still going."

So here she was, and although it was a family

vacation, right now she was alone in the bleachers. Dad was back at the hotel handling a crisis that had come up at work. Mom was browsing the gift store. Her big sister, Grace, was down behind the visiting team's dugout, bouncing on her toes like a little kid. She had a baseball and wanted somebody to sign it. Maya saw one of the men nudge Grace aside to get at the railing. Grace was now stuck in the corner, all but hidden from the players.

Maya felt her shoulders tense up, the way they did whenever she saw someone treated unfairly. She willed somebody to notice her sister. At last a player did. He smiled, signed Grace's baseball, and handed it back. Grace shouted something, probably a flustered thank-you, as the player sprinted off to the outfield. Maya smiled for the first time since she'd gotten to the ballpark. She liked this guy, who had picked her sister out of the crowd.

Grace threaded her way through the crowd and walked along the bleachers to join her.

"What happened to Mom?" she asked.

"She's still at the gift store."

"Like she's going to buy anything."

"I know." Mom was frugal and didn't like baseball.

She must have gotten bored waiting for the game to start. It *was* a long wait. Grace had begged to go early because it was the best time to get autographs. She hadn't expected that there would already be a crowd around the dugout.

"So, who signed your ball?" Maya asked.

"A guy named Rafael." Grace squinted at the signature. "Rafael Ronaldo?"

"Rosales," a voice behind them corrected.

The girls glanced back and saw a man with a spiral-bound notebook on his knee.

"Rosales is the only Rafael on the team," he explained. "He's a non-roster invitee. He was considered one of their hottest prospects, but now he'll be lucky to survive spring training."

"How come?" Maya asked.

"His BA is zero sixty-eight. As in zero point zero six eight."

Maya didn't know much about baseball, but she knew zeroes at the front of a batting average weren't good.

"So maybe he'll get a bunch of hits today," said Grace.

"Probably not a bunch," the guy said, "since he's not in the lineup."

"Of course not," said Grace. "Are you a Twins fan or a Phillies fan?"

"Neither," he said. "I'm a writer. Have you heard of *Sticks and Stitches*? It's a baseball blog."

"Yes," said Grace. "You're Danny Diamond?"

"That's the name they gave me!" he said. "Well, the name I gave myself, obviously. It's my nom de plume. My real name is Danny Rhombus!" He laughed hard at his own joke, then explained. "You see a rhombus is like a…"

"We know," said Grace. She turned back around.

"Kind of a creep," Maya whispered.

"I never liked his blog," said Grace.

* * *

Rosales came in as a pinch hitter late in the game. Maya and Grace stood up and cheered at the top of their lungs as he came to the plate.

"Go, Rafael!" Maya shouted.

"Wallop the ball!" yelled Grace.

Mom didn't know who he was, but she stood because the girls stood, and cheered because they cheered.

"You can do it!"

Rafael glanced back at them. He was young and had a mustache and goatee that looked like he'd drawn them on to look older. Grace held up the ball so he'd remember her. He turned back, dug in, and waited for the first pitch. Maya's heart was beating a little faster than it usually did. She had an urge to look away because she was so worried about this one at bat. So this is what it's like to care about sports, she thought.

Rosales swung and lined the ball past the pitcher's outstretched hand. The shortstop fielded it on the bounce but not in time to throw to first. Rafael sped safely past the base. There was scattered applause around the park.

"Woo-hoo!" Grace shouted.

"Way to go!" Mom yelled.

"Now steal a base!" Maya yelled, surprised at herself.

"It would be stupid to steal second," said the blogger behind them. "They're down by six runs, and there's nobody out."

"Steal it anyway!" shouted Grace. Several people around them laughed. Rafael took a lead off base. The pitcher threw to first; Rafael scampered back in time while the crowd jeered.

"Pitch the ball!"

"Home plate is that way!"

Maya felt a thrill. The other team's pitcher was worried.

The pitcher hurled a fastball toward the plate. Rafael took off for second.

The crowd screamed.

That's not the crowd, Maya realized. *That's me.*

The catcher heaved the ball to second as Rafael tried to slide. The second baseman tagged him on the foot, and the umpire signaled he was out. The crowd groaned.

"That's a CS—for completely stupid," Danny Rhombus announced to nobody as he entered it on his scorecard.

Rafael picked himself up and slinked into the dugout, his uniform now smudged with dirt. Nobody at the dugout door greeted him, told him it was a good effort, or slapped him on the back. Maya didn't care about the out, but it broke her heart that nobody was there to comfort him.

She decided he was her favorite player.

CHAPTER 7

Dad was still at work, hunched over the laptop on the glass coffee table in the living-room half of the suite.

"Did you even have lunch?" Mom asked.

"I grabbed a sub from the place next door." Dad gestured at a sandwich wrapper and paper cup. "How was the game?"

"It was great," said Grace. "Even Maya like it."

"I did have fun," she admitted. But now her worries came swirling back into her head. Especially the bees. Vast numbers of bees were dying, and nobody was sure why.

"We were so close to the players!" said Grace. "I could have spit on Joe Mauer! Not that I would, but that's how close he was!"

"That's awesome," he said. "Wish I could have gone."

But you could have gone, Maya thought. She knew what his work-related emergency was, or at least she had a pretty good idea what it was.

He must have seen her frowning.

"Are you OK, honey?" He reached out and lightly touched the corner of her mouth with his thumb, as if he was going to push it up into a smile.

"Just tired from sitting in the sun," said Maya.

"You do look a little worn out," Dad agreed.

"Dad, what's going on at work?" Grace asked.

"Oh, I don't want to bore you with the details," he said.

"Is Alceria in financial trouble?" she asked in a grave tone. "You can level with us."

"No, no, of course not. Don't worry about us," he said. "We're a very stable company. And don't worry about my job either. Everything is fine. The crisis will be over by the time you get home. I promise." He made a show of shutting the laptop. "Look, I'm done for now."

"Great," said Grace. She eyed the laptop. "Can I have screen time?"

"Sure." Dad pushed the laptop at her. "I'm going to take a dip in the pool before dinner. Do something vacationy on my vacation." He patted Maya's head on his way to the bedroom.

Maya wandered out to the balcony and watched a couple of kids do cannonballs in the kidney-shaped pool. She thought about a fox she'd seen last winter, limping across their snowy front yard one cold morning. When she and Grace had gone to catch their buses, Maya had paused to look at the tracks.

"Are you going to track down the fox and keep it as a pet?" Grace had asked.

"No!" Maya had insisted, although she had been imagining exactly that: following the tracks, discovering the fox curled up underneath the porch of an abandoned house, and carrying it home cradled in her arms. It had seemed so cold and hungry. What was it doing in the middle of the city? Where was its pack? Why was it awake in the middle of winter?

She'd told her father about the fox when he got home from work. They looked up foxes together on the Internet and discovered that foxes were common in the city, even if she'd never seen one before. They found out foxes didn't hibernate when they had plenty of food and didn't mind the cold. They learned that most foxes were solitary and didn't travel in packs like she'd thought. So the fox was fine. Maya was relieved, but a not-very-small part of her was sorry the fox didn't need her.

Baseball players didn't need her either. They were big, strong men with lots of money.

Dad finally trod out to the pool in his trunks and slid into the water. The kids stopped horsing around. Maya went back into the hotel room.

"Hey, let's look up Rafael Rosales on the Internet," she suggested to Grace, who was still on the couch and tapping away on the laptop keyboard.

"Really?" Grace looked up. "You want to look up a baseball player?"

"Sure." She sat down next to Grace, and her sister shifted the computer so Maya could see the screen.

"First baseball crush?" she asked.

"It's not a crush."

"Of course not," said Grace. She entered Rafael's name in the search bar and scanned the results. "I doubt Rafael is also an Argentinian blues guitarist," she said. "Or a graphic arts professor in Rhode Island." She added *baseball* to the search terms. "Aha. Here's a website called DRProspects.com with a whole half-page on our Rafael. That's DR as in Dominican Republic. Lots of baseball players come from there."

"Oh yeah," said Maya, as if she'd known that. She remembered the Dominican Republic from school, one of many island countries in the Caribbean. Two thirds of an island, she corrected herself; the other third was the nation of Haiti.

"It says he's from San Pedro de Ma-cor-ís," Grace sounded out the name. "Listen to this. 'Rosales emerged as one of the top position players in the Dominican Summer League—that's rookie ball—batting .340 and stealing sixteen bases. He is expected to reach A or advanced A next year.'"

"What does that mean?" Maya asked.

"I keep forgetting you don't know *anything*," Grace teased. "When baseball players get drafted, they have to work their way up through the minors. First they play rookie ball, then there's single A, advanced A, double A, and triple A. Every level has its own leagues and its own teams. And every level is a lot harder." She shut the laptop, moved it aside, and put her bare feet on the coffee table.

"Where do the Twins' teams play?"

"All over," said Grace. "Triple A is in New York State, Double A is in Tennessee. Their advanced-A team plays here. They're called the Fort Myers Miracle. Can I have one of those pillows?"

"Sure." Maya handed one to Grace, who set it under her feet.

"Aaah," she said, mimicking their dad perfectly even though she wasn't trying to.

Maya sat sideways on the couch, feet up next to Grace's. She still had a lot of questions.

"So how come Rafael gets to play with the Twins now?" she asked.

"Because it's spring training," said Grace. Her eyes were closed, her head tilted back against the couch. "You don't have to be on the official forty-man roster to play at spring training. Teams can see how their prospects do against major league pitching, or invite old-timers to see if they're washed up or not."

"I get it," said Maya. That Danny guy had said Rafael was a "non-roster invitee." Now she knew that meant he wasn't really a Twin. At least not yet.

"So what will happen to him?"

"I don't know," said Grace. "He could get cut completely or go back to rookie ball in the DR."

"If he starts playing really well, could he skip all that and play in Minnesota this summer?"

"That's not going to happen," said Grace. "He has to develop as a player."

"Next year?"

"Don't count on it."

"What if he never plays for the Twins?" Maya asked.

"He might not," said Grace. "Most minor leaguers never make it to the big leagues."

"Oh," said Maya. She wished she'd known that before she let herself care about his success. She felt hopeless about so many things already.

CHAPTER 8

The next morning, Maya's family went to the beach in the rental car. They got there early enough to park close to the boardwalk. It was lined with tacky gift shops and restaurants advertising all-you-can-eat Gulf shrimp. They trod in their flip-flops across the cool, white sand while seagulls squawked and circled around the surf.

Mom and Dad hid under an umbrella, Mom reading and Dad tapping on his smartphone. Grace attempted to use a boogie board. Maya walked along the surf, letting the waves wash over her feet. Back in Minneapolis, she often felt doomed, seeing the smoke billowing over the skyline and the snowbanks turned gray by exhaust. Here, the water was blue and the beach was littered with shells. Maybe the world would be all right. So much of it was still achingly beautiful. She retreated to the blanket and sat next to her parents, pouring a handful of shells she'd collected from hand to hand. Dad had dozed off.

"Those are pretty," said Mom, looking up from her book to admire the shells. Maya decided she had an opening.

"I was wondering if there are many shellfish left after that oil spill," she said. She knew that a few years ago five million gallons of crude oil had gurgled up from the seafloor, taking their toll on marine life. Her mother sighed wearily as if Maya had been going on and on about the oil spill for days.

"We're having a nice day," she said. "Don't spoil it."

"I wasn't trying to spoil anything," said Maya. "I'm having a nice time." She smiled extra wide to show it was true.

Her mother's voice softened. "I'm glad you care about the world, sweetie. I love that about you. But you have to start filtering or you'll be worried sick all the time."

Maya decided she couldn't tell her mom what was really on her mind.

* * *

That night, when the lights were out, she told Grace.

They were sharing the foldout bed in the living-room part of the hotel suite.

"Alceria is killing bees," she whispered.

"Huh?"

The metal frame of the foldout bed creaked when Maya rolled sideways to look at Grace.

"Alceria make insecticides for crops called neonicotinoids." She had labored over the word, memorizing it in syllables and practicing how to say it. She knew adults and older siblings would jump on a mispronounced word to dismiss a kid's entire argument. "They don't kill bees right away, but the poison affects their central nervous system and they get lost and then they die. When enough bees die, the whole colony collapses." Maya went on, now blurting out details in a nonlinear way. If the bees died, fresh fruit and flowers couldn't get pollinated. If that happened, people would starve. And even if it didn't happen, the bees were part of the ecosystem. A keystone species, they were called. Because without them, the entire system collapsed.

"Where did you learn all this?" Grace asked.

"TV."

"One of those nature documentaries? They always say the sky is falling."

"No, it was *60 Minutes*. I was flipping through the channels last week and saw it." That wasn't true. She'd known it was going to be on and tuned in on purpose.

Grace said nothing.

"So, Dad's a part of it," Maya added. "He's part of Alceria."

"Dad sits in an office all day. How is he killing bees?"

"He helps Alceria, and Alceria kills bees."

"Well, I'm sure he's against it," said Grace. "It's not like he gets to decide what the whole company does."

"No, of course not." But Maya wasn't sure. Dad had smoked out a hornet's nest once, and they were almost the same thing as bees. She continued. "I think that's his crisis at work," she said. "This show aired a few days ago, and now Dad's trying to make the data tell a different story, even if it's not the true story."

"Dad is not a liar," said Grace.

"I didn't say he was," said Maya.

"Actually, you did." Grace rolled over, turning her back to Maya. Maya waited for Grace to calm down, to turn back around and talk some more, but a few moments later she was asleep.

CHAPTER 9

Maya woke before dawn. Grace had kicked around and rolled herself diagonally across the bed, leaving Maya crammed into an isosceles triangle. She climbed out of bed, used the toilet, and washed up in the clam-shaped sink. She saw in the mirror that the tops of her ears were bright red. She'd forgotten to put sunscreen there. She touched the burn on one ear and watched it turn white and then red again. Why did it do that? She could ask Dad. He was like her own personal Bill Nye the Science Guy, explaining why ice froze and how airplanes flew.

When she came out of the bathroom, she saw a rectangle of blue light in the alcove by the door. She thought for a moment that Grace had woken up and gotten online, but Maya saw the hump of Grace's body was still on the foldout bed. It was Dad. She walked over to ask him about the strange properties of sunburns.

"Hi," he said sheepishly. He'd pulled over a chair and had his feet up on an empty suitcase. "Hope I didn't wake you up."

"You didn't. But Dad, are you working? It's like four a.m."

"I know. I have a few things to catch up on. And I couldn't sleep anyway."

Maya forgot all about sunburns. "Dad, is any of this about the story on *60 Minutes*?"

He looked at her with startled eyes. "You saw it?"
She nodded.

"Yes, that's the crisis," he admitted. "Although the official phrase at Alceria is 'an opportunity for strategic communication.'" Maya snickered at the doublespeak.

"Thanks for telling me," she said. At least he was talking to her like a grown-up.

"Don't worry about it, sweetheart." He closed the laptop. "My job is safe. Alceria isn't going to collapse overnight."

"But...but..." she stammered. "Dad, I'm worried about the *bees*."

"Honey, the media… Well, fear gets better ratings than facts. That's all."

"They did have facts. They had numbers. They had a scientist on from the U named Dr. Jenkins. All she does is study bees!"

"Look," he interrupted. "I'm the grown-up here, and I'm the one with a college degree and twelve years of experience in agribusiness. I think I know more about this than you do."

Maya's shoulders tensed up. Dad wasn't talking to her like an adult anymore.

"Maya, we worry about *you* because of the way you worry about…well, bees and polar bears." He reached out and gently combed hair out of her face with his fingers. "Honey, the adults haven't broken everything as much as you think they have."

Maya saw how rumpled and unshaven her dad was, how rimmed his eyes were with redness. Now she was worried about him too. She decided she wouldn't bring up the bees anymore.

* * *

They had a late lunch at a restaurant near the airport, one with fishing nets strewn along the walls. The restaurant was busy even though it was late for lunch and early for dinner. The heaping plates of fried shrimp made Maya wonder if any were left in the Gulf.

Baseball fans in red jerseys were sitting at a table talking about the game that afternoon. Maya felt a tug of regret: her own family could have squeezed another game in before they flew home. She wanted to stand in the bleachers and cheer with her sister beside her.

Grace had barely spoken to her all day. Even when Maya asked if the Twins won yesterday, Grace pretended not to hear. But now her sister elbowed her in a chummy way.

"Look at the bar," she whispered, her lips barely moving.

Maya glanced over and saw the baseball blogger from the stadium. He was drinking a king-sized beer and eating a plate of crab legs. He had a laptop open on the bar next to him and was clattering on the keys in between bites.

"It's your boyfriend," Maya whispered.

Grace snickered and rolled her eyes. "You're the future Mrs. Rhombus," she teased. They were acting like the mean girls in middle school, but at least they were getting along. Danny noticed them on their way out and waved. Maya waved back since he was being friendly.

"Were you at the game?" he asked.

"No," she said.

"I've got an interview lined up," he said. "I better not tell you who it is with, but if you stick around, you won't be sorry. I'll tell you that much."

"We're about to fly back to Minnesota, actually."

"Well," he said, "you might run into your friend Rafael Rosales at the airport."

"Huh?"

"He's gone," he explained, scissoring his fingers through the air like he was cutting a thread. "They sent him back to the Dominican Republic. You can tell him *hasta luego*, but it might be more like *hasta nunca*." He shrugged. "My condolences."

If Grace hadn't reached back to grab her elbow and pull her toward the door, Maya might have dumped the king-sized beer on Danny Rhombus's head.

CHAPTER 10

Rafael, Nine Years Ago

The sugar farm where Papa worked shut down forever after the harvest. Papa said it was because the price of sugar dropped. The owners couldn't keep the place going even with their lousy wages and never buying new equipment.

It happened a few weeks after Christmas. That was good timing because the Three Kings had already given Rafael the real baseball glove he'd asked for. His birthday wasn't until August. Dad might have a new job by then, but Rafael couldn't count on it.

"What'll happen to the girl with the chicken?" Iván whispered to Rafael that night.

Rafael had not forgotten the little girl at the batey, but he was surprised Iván remembered. They'd only seen her once for a few seconds.

"You should worry about us," said Rafael. "Papa lost his job, you know."

"Papa will get a new job," said Iván.

"So will that girl's parents," said Rafael. "There's other cane to cut."

"But the other sugar farms are far away," said Iván. "It's a long way to carry a chicken."

"She'll be all right," said Rafael. "They'll both be all right."

"I hope we see her again," said Iván. He paused. "When you're a rich and famous baseball player like Sammy Sosa, can they come live with us in your mansion?"

"Of course."

"Including the chicken?"

"The chicken will have its own room," said Rafael.

* * *

Papa couldn't find another job as a mechanic. He opened a shop inside the house and started fixing appliances.

"Those are completely different from the machines you're used to," Rafael's mother said, worried. But Papa patted her hand. "It's fine. All machines are the same. I can tell how things work by looking at them." Soon the house was crowded with broken televisions and radios.

"Let me show you how this works," Papa said one day to Rafael. It was summer, and Rafael was home but restless and bored. Papa had the front panel off a coffeemaker, a fancy one with a dozen buttons, and was studying the tangle of wires inside. "You're almost ten, and you're ready to learn a trade. Let me show you how to fix things so you always have work."

Rafael tried to concentrate, but his mind wandered outside to the street where he heard laughter and cheering. Something was going on. Something bigger than the usual game of streetball.

"See here, a broken wire. Five minutes to fix," Papa told him. "You can even use bits and pieces from other machines. It's very easy." Papa nimbly twisted wires and wrapped them with black tape. His hands were big but could handle small things. "See?" He replaced the panel, plugged in the pot, and found that the light-up display still didn't work. Papa cursed, removed the panel again, and saw a new smoldering of melted plastic. "Everything is more complicated than it needs to be!" he complained, poking at what looked like a circuit board. "Why does a coffeemaker need a computer?"

The noise from outside was even greater. There were so many voices and so much clapping and stamping that it sounded like Tetelo Vargas stadium. Papa didn't seem to notice.

"Can I go outside?" Rafael asked.

"Fine, you go outside," Papa muttered. "You go play games, and I'll break everything I am supposed to be fixing!" Rafael knew his father was being sarcastic, but he was dying to find out what was going on. He jumped off his chair.

"Where are you going?" his mother asked. Rafael had barely noticed she was there, but now she appeared in his path, wagging her finger. "Your father is trying to teach you. It's important to him that you learn."

"But I don't want to fix machines," Rafael protested.

He was braced for a fight, but his mother crouched down, took him into a fierce hug that squeezed the breath out of him, and whispered in his ear as she did so: "Your father needs you to believe in him, Rafael."

He knew what she meant. She wanted him to stay. But the excitement in the street was too much to ignore. He pulled away from her.

"I believe in you, Papa!" Rafael shouted, and darted out the door.

He had never seen so many kids in the street at once. They must have poured in from every corner of the barrio and were crowding around the spot where they played streetball.

"What's going on?" he asked a boy he didn't know.

"Rogério Romero is here!"

Rafael's heart skipped a beat. There was a real, live major leaguer right here in front of his house. Not only a major leaguer, an all-star! He leaped into the fray, overwhelmed by the need to shake hands with this man, to feel the magic in his hands. He had a feeling that Rogério would recognize the same magic in Rafael, would give him a knowing look and say, "I'll see you in the big time."

He wormed his way to the front and saw that inside the mob was a circle of sawhorses. Inside the circle, Rogério had a hand on Juan's shoulder and another on his throwing hand, showing him his famous cutter grip. Also inside the circle were men with cameras and microphones, and other men who kept the crowd back.

Rafael felt sick. If he had been playing today, Rogério Romero might have picked him to teach a cutter grip for the camera. The lesson had ended, and now they let another dozen boys gather around Rogério for a photo. Rafael was not quick enough to be one of them. Rogério crouched as the boys crowded around and put his long arms around their shoulders. There were snaps and flashes of photography.

One of the other men handed Rogério a big canvas sports bag, and he started to dole out baseballs. "Don't use this in the street," he told the first boy he handed a ball to, a boy who was not even part of their games. "You might break a window." The boy smiled and nodded and held up the ball proudly for the camera. The worst was yet to come. Rogério reached deeper into the bag and came up with a Dodgers cap.

"We have to fix this problem!" he said. He took the Yankees cap off Juan's head, replaced it with the Dodgers cap, and tamped it down on his head.

"Who's your team now?" he asked.

"Los Dodgers!"

The men laughed and the boys cheered and the camera moved in for a close-up of Rogério's big, happy face and Juan's, arms around each other like best friends.

He stole this from me, Rafael thought, against all reason. Juan stole this from me.

To see another boy live his own dream cut into Rafael like a blade. *No hay mal que por bien no venga*, he reminded himself: good always came from the bad, like the sweet juice pouring out of cut cane. The good thing to come from this badness was that Juan started playing at the field by the taxi stand. Juan saw him walking there with Hugo one day; Juan had the brim of his Dodgers cap pulled down to shade his face, the way Rogério Romero wore his.

Juan's absence meant that Rafael could at least play streetball. He sneaked out the house one morning before anyone else was awake and found Tomás and Diego and another boy practicing over by the old factory. They didn't have enough players yet for a game.

"Can I play?" Rafael asked.

"*Claro*," said Tomás. "If you play on my team."

"Where have you been?" Diego asked.

"I've been helping my papa. Learning his business." Rafael puffed up his chest a bit, feeling grown up, even though he hadn't learned a thing.

"Go get your brother," said Diego. "He should play too."

"Really?" Had Diego forgotten what happened the last time Iván played?

"Really! My brother Eddie is playing now." He gestured at the boy Rafael didn't know. "He knows Iván from school and wants him to play."

"Maybe tomorrow." Rafael's father would be awake by now and would rope Rafael back into helping him work.

Other boys came along, and soon they had enough players for two teams.

It felt great to swing at a ball and connect, to see the ball hop past the pitcher, and to hear the laughter and shouts of other boys as Rafael sprinted to the base. It was exhilarating to chase after a ball and catch it on the bounce, whirl around and fire it to Tomás as he tagged the base. He liked how Eddie watched him and imitated his moves. Maybe it wouldn't be so bad to have Iván here too.

When Rafael got home for lunch, his father had cleared off the table, but the guts of some device were piled in the corner. Papa barely looked at Iván as they ate their *bandera*. Rafael had skipped breakfast and was ravenous. He gobbled up his rice and beans and asked for more.

"You were out playing ball?" his father finally asked as he pushed his chair back from the table.

Rafael nodded; his mouth was too full to speak.

"It's understandable," his father said. "Boys need to play, but you can help me this afternoon."

Rafael gulped some water to wash his food down. They used to buy water in jugs, but now Mama boiled tap water on the stove until it was safe to drink. It tasted of metal.

"I could use another set of hands," said Papa.

"The others are expecting me to play ball," said Rafael.

Papa looked at him with lowered eyebrows. Rafael met his gaze. He realized that his father really wanted him to stay. If Papa had said he missed Rafael and wanted him around, not to learn a trade but simply to be together, Rafael would have not been able to say no.

But his father stood and picked up his plate.

"I know how it is," he said. "To do what is expected of you."

* * *

"The other boys asked about you," he told Iván that night. "Do you want to play tomorrow?"

"Last time you yelled at me."

That had been months ago and felt like years to Rafael.

"You got in my way. Anyway, you hit another kid with the bat!"

"He called you a name."

"I promise I won't yell at you again unless you hit somebody with a stick."

"I promise I won't hit anybody unless I have a stick."

Rafael guffawed. "Then I guess you don't get to bat."

"I'll play if I can be on your team," said Iván.

"Of course."

"And if you yell, I'll quit."

"I won't yell."

So the next day Iván walked with Rafael to the cul-de-sac. Rafael insisted on being a *capitán* and picked Iván first. Diego picked Tomás.

"Eddie!" Iván insisted. "Pick Eddie!"

"Fine. Eduardo." Eddie came over, and Daniel joined Tomás and Diego. That made the teams uneven, with older boys on one side. Rafael decided this would be a good day to not keep score.

Rafael would have to pitch. "You be catcher," he told Iván. "If a player is coming home, be ready to catch the ball and tag him out."

"I know. I know."

He didn't know though and was not paying attention when the first run scored. Eddie tried his best to field, but he was too small to catch up with a lot of the hard-hit balls. Rafael remembered his promise not to yell and bit his tongue. The three older boys batted three or four times each before they made three outs.

When they finally came up to bat, Rafael let Iván go first. His little brother swung at everything. Nothing was looser in streetball than the number of strikes that made an out; it was especially high for the smaller boys, but after ten or eleven swings, Iván himself gave up.

"I don't want to hit anymore."

"You have to," said Rafael. "That's part of the game."

"I don't want to," said Iván. He looked close to tears. "I don't know how."

"Watch me," said Rafael. He took the stick and took practice swings.

"You move too fast," said Iván.

"I'll slow down."

"You watch too," Diego told his brother. "Rafael is the best hitter I know." He lobbed a soft pitch, one Rafael should have creamed. Rafael anchored his foot, pulled his weight back, and swung. He tried to do it slowly but lost his balance and stumbled.

"Nice lesson!" Daniel teased from behind the plate.

Rafael tried to laugh it off. "I was showing them how to whiff." He missed a second time, swinging ahead of the pitch because he was so eager to prove himself. The boys laughed again. Rafael muttered to himself. He wouldn't miss this time. He would scorch the ball past Tomás and into the street beyond. He would show them. Iván looked at him, his eyes full of hope. He wanted Rafael to show them too.

"Throw it faster," he told Diego.

Diego threw it faster. Rafael froze and watched the ball sail past him. He dropped the stick. He would give anything to have that moment back. Plenty of boys got extra pitches, but he didn't dare ask.

He didn't think it was possible for the moment

to get worse, but it did. He glanced up and saw Juan Santos Garcia, back from the baseball field, wearing his Dodgers cap and smiling a lopsided smile.

CHAPTER 12

Rafael stormed past Juan without a word. Iván hurried to keep up.

"What happened?" Iván asked. "Did you strike out?"

"What do you think?" Rafael snapped. He turned around and saw Iván stopped in his tracks, his eyes damp.

"Come on," said Rafael. He took a deep breath and let it out slowly. "I'm sorry I yelled."

"It's not that," he said.

"What then?"

"I'm sad you struck out," said Iván.

"It's no big deal," said Rafael. "Everybody strikes out sometimes."

"You don't."

"Sure I do," said Rafael. "David Ortiz strikes out.

Vladimir Guerrero strikes out. I strike out too. Don't worry. I'll be fine."

But he wasn't fine.

After that day, everything he did with the bat felt wrong. He was too aware of his knees and elbows. His feet seemed to slide around on the asphalt. He swung early or swung late. He hit balls that dribbled back to the pitcher or flew back over his own head. The worst part was knowing that Iván was watching him, his eyes full of hope, and Rafael was letting him down every time.

"I'm not going to play anymore," Iván said after a couple of weeks.

"I haven't yelled at you since that first game," Rafael reminded him.

"I know," said Iván. "But you're the one who's going to be the famous baseball player. Papa is going to teach me how to fix things, and I'm going to help him."

"He said that you could?" Iván was only six. How was he going to help?

"It was his idea."

"Wow." Rafael felt a mixture of relief and regret. Papa must have given up on teaching *him* anything. "Do you want to fix things?" he asked.

"I want to make a living," said Iván. "Papa says people always break things, and they will always need people to fix them."

"Papa is smart," said Rafael.

"Rafi," said Iván. "You should ask that older boy to help you out of your slump."

"Diego or Tomás?"

"The one I fought with that time. He's good, right?"

"You mean Juan. Yes, he is very good." Rafael had bitter feelings toward Juan but couldn't deny that the older boy could play baseball. He was also good at showing other boys how to do things. But Rafael couldn't ask because Juan was so arrogant, with his Dodgers cap and hotshot big brother. He couldn't ask because Juan had called him a gallina in front of the other boys. He couldn't ask because Juan had hogged Rogério Romero's time. He couldn't ask because Juan acted like the boss of everyone. He couldn't ask because everything about Juan made him sick with jealousy.

"I can't ask Juan for help," said Rafael. "He hates me."

* * *

When Rafael got up the next morning, his father had already cleared the table and laid out a big sheet of white paper. Rafael sat down at the far end of the table to eat his breakfast of mashed plantain and mango. His father laid out screws and bolts and other parts of the portable stereo he was disassembling. Iván climbed up into a chair and watched.

"Today we learn the basics," said Papa.

"*Aprendemos las bases*," Iván echoed. Rafael's ears tuned in.

"First, we lay things out in the order we remove them," said Papa. "So we don't forget which order to put them back."

"*Sentamos las cosas en orden*," said Iván.

"Don't put your elbows on the table. You might shake things and make them roll."

"*No codos en la mesa*," said Iván, shifting back in his chair.

Rafael watched, feeling strange. His father had never gone over these fundamentals with him, had never gone to the trouble of teaching him the *bases*. Papa had only haphazardly included him in things once they were underway.

It's because he knew I didn't care, Rafael told himself, but a deeper feeling gnawed at him. Papa didn't think I would try. He thought it was a waste of time to teach me at all, and I proved he was right.

But it didn't matter, because he would be a famous baseball player. He would buy a big house for his parents, one with more rooms than they knew what to do with, and a swimming pool and a garage with a big car. He imagined walking Papa and Mama through the house, letting them admire all the fine new appliances and shiny fixtures, and then telling them, as a surprise, that the house was not his, but theirs. His father would look at him with teary eyes, feeling grateful but also sorry that he hadn't believed in Rafael earlier.

But there would be no million-US-dollar baseball bonuses and no expensive houses if he couldn't even play streetball. Rafael left the house, but instead of going to the streetball game, he walked the other way. He hurried past the colmado and past the tiny vacant lot where he had once played pirates with Iván. He ran across the busy Calle Mir and kept walking, his heart pounding. He was not supposed to go this far from home by himself. A few minutes later, the road broke left. The campo was on the right.

He had seen it before, driving past it with his father. There was a chain-link fence all the way around the field. There was practically no foul territory and no room for bleachers. The field was mostly dirt, but the baselines were straight and measured, the outfield wide, and there was netting behind home plate. This was real baseball. A row of spectators, mostly boys, now straddled the fence. Rafael found a spot and clambered up.

"Hola," said the boy next to him.

"Hola. I heard Rogério Romero used to play here," Rafael told him.

"Everybody knows that," said the boy. "Also Tonio Mendez, who plays for the Pirates."

"Wow. Do you ever play?"

"No. I'm not good. I like to watch."

Rafael rested his feet in the diamonds of the fence and tried to get comfortable. There were no dugouts. The players waiting to bat leaned against the fence behind the backstop. They had real bats, a mix of banged-up wooden ones and metal ones. Most of the boys had gloves, however old and battered. And the pitcher was hurling a real ball.

Rafael searched for Juan and didn't see him. He did see Hugo in the row of boys waiting to bat. Perhaps Juan was in the outfield. The boys there were too far away to recognize.

The boy now batting sailed a foul ball to left field. The left fielder ran after it. Rafael could only see his silhouette against the morning sun, but knew by the way he moved that it was Juan. He recognized the body, the stride, and the way he crooked his neck. Juan leaped into the air and caught the ball for an out, then whipped it back to the pitcher on one bounce. The boys on the fence hooted and cheered, and Rafael realized he was cheering along with them. Instead of the sick jealous feeling he was used to, he felt a swell of pride.

"That's my friend Juan," he told the boy next to him. "We used to play streetball together."

A moment later he wished he hadn't said it, because Juan's catch was the third out. The players came in from the field to bat. They lined up near Rafael and the other boy. Since he'd claimed Juan was a pal, he now had to say hello. What if Juan scoffed at him or, worse, ignored him completely? What if he threw back a casual "Oh hi" as if Rafael was not even worth ignoring, merely another boy on the fence?

He could have lain low and hoped Juan wouldn't see him, but now he was stuck.

"Juan..." he started but found his voice too weak to

carry over the chatter. He cleared his throat and found his voice deep inside him. "Juan! Great catch!"

Juan turned and saw him. He cracked his familiar grin, came over, grabbed Rafael's hand, and practically pulled him off the fence.

"This is the one," he told his teammates. "This is the boy I told you about. He has *la intensidad* like nobody I ever played with. Even in streetball, he would make me ashamed for goofing off."

Rafael could have burst with pride.

"We need you, *mi amigo*, to keep these guys from counting clouds in the outfield." Juan threw his arms around two older boys. "Rafael, you should play with us."

CHAPTER 13

The teams were already decided for the morning, but Juan promised Rafael could play next time.

"Get here early tomorrow!" he said.

"Your house is on the way," Rafael said. "I'll meet you."

"*Excelente!*"

Rafael returned to his spot on the fence. He held on tight, for fear he would float away.

"Do you know his brother too?" the boy next to him asked.

"Hugo. Of course," Rafael said. He was now brimming with confidence. "I've been to their house."

"He will be a superstar," said the boy.

"Everybody knows it," Rafael agreed.

The game resumed. Maybe next time, Rafael would

play too. It was hard to believe.

He had not forgotten he couldn't hit anymore. He also knew Juan was one boy of many—the youngest boy playing, probably—and his word alone wouldn't be enough to get Rafael into a game. But it didn't matter. What mattered was that Rafael had a plan. He would work with Juan to get his swing back. Then he would play here with the big boys and show his intensity.

The boys played more seriously than Rafael was used to, but they were not completely competitive. At one point, the pitcher talked to a batter about how to hit his own pitches. When the second baseman muffed a play, both teams gathered around the base for a discussion of how he should have played it. They were playing to get better, not to win.

The game ended on a tie, after five and a half innings, because it was time for lunch. Rafael fell into step with Hugo and Juan.

"Where have you been?" Juan asked.

"I was helping my papa. He has a repair shop."

The street was especially busy. Shuttle buses full of tourists drove slowly by, giving the passengers a tour of the city. Motor scooters zipped around them. A woman in a straw hat led a mule drawing a wagon full of fruits and vegetables.

"Right. Diego said you started playing again a couple of weeks ago."

"Yeah, but I'm rusty."

They ran across the street. A truck bleated at them, even though they had the light on their side.

"I need help batting," said Rafael. "Can we practice after lunch?"

"Sure," said Juan. "We should do that. *Hasta pronto!*" He followed Hugo into their house.

Rafael realized he was late for lunch. His mother must have called for him, perhaps even sent Iván out looking for him. He hoped he wasn't in trouble. He hurried home and saw his mother by the stove looking upset.

"Sorry I'm late," he said.

"Your father won't let us eat anyway," his mother grumbled.

"We're almost finished. Relax." His father slid a panel back into place on a cassette recorder. Iván was on his knees in a chair, watching intently. Papa held out a hand, and Iván dropped a small screw into his palm. His father screwed it into one corner of the panel and held out his hand for another, then another.

Iván delivered each screw as if he were assisting a brain surgeon.

"People in the United States throw things away that are almost new," Papa said. "Things that are easy to fix, like this. All I had to do was tighten the chassis." Rafael held his breath when his father pressed Play on the machine. A Puerto Rican rap song blared out of the speakers. The machine did not rattle.

"It's good!" Iván threw his arms in the air.

"Oh, this song," said their mother, shaking her head in disapproval.

"*A ella le gusta la gasolina*!" Papa sang. He took Mama's hands and made her dance, turning circles between the kitchen and the dining area, her still holding a wooden spoon.

Iván leaped off the chair and joined in, and Rafael did the same. The four of them danced around as if lunch wasn't getting cold, there were no other machines to fix, and nothing on earth was left to worry about.

CHAPTER 14

Maya

On the second Saturday in April, Maya went into the backyard to rip up sod. Her family had a big yard, but it was shabby and weedy compared to the other neatly maintained lawns along Victory Memorial Drive. She'd already staked out the long rectangle—fifteen feet by five—where she would place her garden, and now she had to prepare it for planting. She grabbed a shovel and hacked out a square in the sod, then pried up the grassy surface. It was harder than she thought. Spring had come to the sky, but the ground was stuck in winter. After an hour, she rested her elbow on the shovel handle and looking at the work in front of her. It would be easier and more fun if she had help.

Grace came out of the back door.

"So, you're really doing this native weeds thing?"

"Native grasses and forbs," Maya corrected, once again plunging the shovel into the ground and placing her foot on the blade.

"What's a forb?"

Maya pried up the sod, leaving Grace's question unanswered for a moment. She relished a moment of knowing something her big sister did not.

"Well?"

"The stuff that grows on grasslands that isn't grass," said Maya, as she dropped the sod on the pile. "Like thistle and dandelions."

"Yeah. The rest of us call those weeds," said Grace.

"A weed is a plant you don't want. I want these, so they aren't weeds."

"What," said Grace, "ever."

Maya turned up another strip of sod and saw a big grub, mealy white in the morning sun. She gritted her teeth and refused to be grossed out. It's a baby beetle, she reminded herself. Who doesn't like babies?

"Want to help?"

Grace made a face. "I think I'll pass. Besides, I don't want to get sweaty. I'm going to hang out with Rachel."

"Are you going all the way to Woodbury?" Maya

asked. Grace's best friend had moved across the Twin Cities last year.

"I'm hoping we can meet halfway so I'm not on a bus all day," said Grace. She let out a breath. "I cannot *wait* until I get a driver's license."

Maya shoveled up some soil and gently covered the grub. Some beetles were good for the garden, eating the bugs that ate the plants. She hoped this one was that kind.

"Anyway, I thought you might like to know something," said Grace, but she did not go on. Maya set her shovel down again.

"Know what?"

"It's not as interesting as forbs," Grace said. "But the Twins rookie team in the DR updated their roster."

"And?"

"You've been checking a couple of times a day to see if Rafael is on it, so…"

"Yes I have. So tell me!"

"Hold on." Grace bent over and scratched her ankle. She was obviously getting even with Maya for stalling on the explanation of forbs.

"Grace!"

"He's on the roster," Grace finally said, grinning. "He hasn't been cut."

"Oh, yay!" Maya raised the shovel triumphantly.

"It says the roster is *tentative*," said Grace, drawing out the last word. "And since he's in his third year now…"

"I know, I know." She and Grace had read into the rules for the rookie leagues. Players had to move up by the end of their third season or get cut, and really only had until July, when the teams would have to make room for the newest players after the international draft.

"He's still got a shot," said Grace. "Well, have fun shoveling. I'm going to go call Rachel."

The good news gave Maya a burst of energy. She dug until her shoulders hurt, humming a pop song, thinking about baseball and bees. She took another break and admired her work. She had cleared nearly a fifth of the garden. There was no way she could finish today, she realized, but since flowers bloomed at different times, she could plant it gradually over the spring and summer.

Her father now came out of the house, wearing the beaten shoes he wore when he mowed the lawn.

"You know, I could rent a sod cutter," he said.

"I know," said Maya. She'd read articles on the Internet about turning lawn into garden. "It just seems like a lot for something this small." It also seemed like starting off on the wrong foot—saving the planet by using a machine that burned gasoline.

"Maybe so," he said. "Want me to dig a row?"

"Really?

"Sure. I'm kind of geeked about this prairie garden."

"Yes. Please. Thank you." She handed him the shovel and he began to dig, working at twice her speed.

"Your mom's ready to go to the garden center," he said. "Do you want to shower first?"

"Uh. Is that a hint?"

He said nothing, and she guessed it was a hint. She was coated in sweat and dirt.

"I am pretty gross," she admitted. "I'll go clean up."

"I wouldn't say gross," said Dad. "Grubby. I'd say grubby."

Inside, Mom was sitting on the couch, paging through the flyer from the garden center.

"How's your garden coming along?"

"Good," said Maya. "Dad's helping."

"He's pretty geeked about this prairie thing," said Mom.

"That's what he said. I'm going to take a quick shower before we go."

"OK. Be quick. I want to get groceries too."

As she showered, Maya imagined the plants full grown and flowering, humming with fuzzy visitors. That was the real reason for the garden: to draw bees with native wildflowers and give them a safe place to collect pollen. But the bees were still a touchy issue with Dad. It was much easier to call her garden a little pocket of prairie.

* * *

After she was dried and dressed, Maya popped into the office area she shared with Grace. She wanted to see the DSL Twins roster with her own eyes, and Grace was still on the phone with Rachel so she actually had a chance. She noticed the open browser window, and the title caught her eye: *A Thinking Girl's Baseball Blog.*

She started reading the top entry:

> Thinking Girl has two opinions about the benches-clearing tussle in B-more last night. One is that we don't need any more GIFs from the brawl with funny captions, and the other is that we don't need any more "analysis" of Armijo's short temper. (That plays a bit too much to the "hot-blooded Latino" stereotype

for TG.) Thinking Girl would rather talk about
the blown save itself, already Armijo's third
this season, and what it means for his future...

This was the kind of blog Grace always read. The only difference was that a woman wrote it instead of some
know-it-all blowhard like Danny Rhombus. Maya had
nearly clicked away when she saw a note at the bottom.

In other news, Fledgling Fan is delighted to
discover that her minor-league crush object
has not been sent packing. News from the
DR is that FF's MLCO will be on the rookie-
league roster despite a deplorable spring that
put a big question mark on his future.

Maya blinked.

Fledgling Fan...minor-league crush object...news
from the DR...deplorable spring...

She clicked back through older posts. Entry after
entry, there was more about this Fledgling Fan and her
minor-league crush. Someone sure seemed to be writing
about her and Rafael, and that could only be one girl
slash baseball fan.

CHAPTER 15

"Yeah, so I have a blog," said Grace, who'd stepped up behind her without Maya noticing. "That's what I get for not shutting my browser window."

"You made fun of me." Maya spun the office chair around with a squeal.

"Huh?"

"Fledgling fan? Minor-league crush object?" She stood up so she could get in Grace's face. "I can't believe you'd talk about me like that to strangers!"

Grace backed up. "It's not like anybody knows it's you. They don't even know my real name. And they're not strangers; they're friends."

"Ha!" said Maya. "If they don't know your name, they're strangers!"

"You don't know how these things work."

"Are you ready to go?" Mom called from downstairs.

"Coming!" Maya called back, then whispered: "Take all of the stuff about me off, or I'm telling."

"Telling what?"

"That you have a blog."

"Go ahead," said Grace. "It's not a big secret or anything." She moved past Maya to get to the office chair.

"I bet Mom and Dad don't know about it though," said Maya. "And they definitely don't know you're talking about *me*."

"And I bet Dad doesn't know about the real reason for your native frobs," said Grace.

"Forbs," said Maya acidly, missing Grace's point. "They're called forbs."

"You mean bee magnets," said Grace, which took the wind out of Maya. "I'm not the only one who forgets to close browser tabs. You're turning our yard into a resort for stinging bugs."

"Maya!" Mom called again.

"Why don't you add a mosquito grotto while you're at it?" Grace said. "Or a cockroach villa in the basement?"

"Shut up! You don't know anything! And you're a cyberbully!" Maya stalked down the hall, pretending she didn't hear Grace's snort of laughter at her use of that word. She felt such a mishmash of things that she could barely sort it out. Was that the way Grace really thought of her? As a baby bird with a crush?

* * *

When Maya got home, Dad was in the family room watching the Masters Golf Tournament—one of the few sporting events he watched every year. She stood for a moment, liking the pan shots of the beautiful greenery until she realized the whole course was probably drenched in insecticides.

"Hey, Rodney called about babysitting," said Dad. "He's going back to work and needs someone to take Claire after school. He said to email."

"Oh. Great." Rodney was a former coworker of her mom's who lived in the neighborhood. Now he was a stay-at-home dad with a toddler named Claire. Rodney had paid Maya a couple of times to play with Claire while he did work around the house. That was easy, because Rodney would swoop in whenever Claire got moody or needed a pull-up change. Being all alone with her would be way different.

Maya found Grace on the computer, as always.

"I need to use the computer," she said.

"I'm busy," said Grace. "In case you can't tell."

"You've been on it all day! I only need it for five minutes."

"Well, you could at least ask nicer." Grace closed her browser window and opened a new one for Maya. As she brushed by, Maya felt enough friction to start a fire.

She took her time writing a message to Rodney, trying to sound professional even though he'd known her when she was a baby. She told him she was very interested in babysitting and looked forward to seeing Claire again. After sending the email, she navigated to Grace's blog to see if she'd deleted the stuff about her.

She hadn't deleted a thing, and there was a new post.

Erratum: Fledgling Fan wants you all to know that her interest in the rookie from the DR is not a "crush." She sees him more as a puppy in the rain. Out of respect for her and the truth, MLCO will now stand for minor-league compassion object.

"No," she said aloud. "Grace!"

Grace came back in, still bristling with negative energy.

"I want you to delete this stuff about me. Including the last post. Especially the last post. I don't see Rafael as a *puppy*." Something about that really irritated her.

Grace let out an exasperated groan. "Well, I need to get on the computer if I'm going to take down half my blog history."

When Maya stood, she saw her sister's eyes were full of anger and hurt.

"So, um, what happened to Rachel? I mean, today."

"None of your business," Grace fumed.

Maya slinked into her room. Mom and Dad had redone her room for her eleventh birthday. The walls were light blue, with an art print of animal-shaped clouds and a mobile of dangling songbirds. Her mother had picked out a plush green rug. Maya had barely thought about it at the time—a rug was a rug—but came to love squishing her bare feet in it, or lying on it while she read or daydreamed. It was like lying on a patch of perfect grass under a perfect sky. She did so now and felt her frustration with Grace turn to happier thoughts.

Babysitting money would help pay for the garden, the garden would help the bees, and the bees would help the world. Rafael Rosales was still playing baseball. It was going to be a great spring and summer, she decided.

She was at peace again. Her room had that effect on her.

CHAPTER 16

Maya felt very grown-up picking up Claire from the Montessori on Monday. It was three blocks from her own school and two blocks from Claire's house. As they walked home, Claire was adorable, tugging on Maya's hand and singing a song to herself. This will be easy, Maya thought.

"Do you need to use the potty?" she asked when they got inside. Rodney and Seth—Claire's other dad—said Claire was out of pull-ups now but needed constant prompting.

"No! I don't have to use the potty!"

"Just sit on it and try."

"Nooooooo!" Claire wailed like a siren. She jumped on the couch and threw a pillow at Maya.

"All right, all right," said Maya. "You don't have

to." Another pillow flew at her and missed. Claire ran out of pillows and started to kick at her from the couch.

What have I gotten myself into? Maya thought.

"How about a snack?" she suggested. "I think there are gummy bears..."

For some reason, that set off the Claire siren again.

"Nooooooo! I don't want gummy bears! I hate gummy bears!"

"OK, let's take five," said Maya. It was something Mom and Dad used to do with her when she was little. She hadn't thought of it in years. She held up a hand and counted to five with her fingers while taking a deep breath. She then counted down and exhaled.

Claire followed along out of curiosity and a few seconds later was calm.

Maybe I can do this, thought Maya.

"*Curious George* is on right now," Claire announced, and sat on the floor of the living room in front of the TV. Maya would have loved to let Claire zone out for a while, but Claire's dads had said no TV. How does she know Curious George is on right now if she never watches TV? Maya wondered, but then she dismissed the thought.

"Do you want to practice letters?" she asked, grabbing a pad of paper and a bucket of crayons and sitting down on the floor.

"*A B C D E G H J...*" Claire shouted cheerfully, missing a few letters.

"No, I mean writing them out," said Maya, but Claire shouted the alphabet again.

"Can I tell you about my bee garden?" Maya asked.

Claire's mouth dropped open. "You grow bees?"

"Sort of." Maya drew flowers on the blank page. "I grow flowers, and the bees live there because of the flowers," she said. The flower hadn't bloomed yet, and she hadn't seen one bee, but Claire didn't need to know that.

"Draw the bees!"

"Of course." Maya added a dozen yellow smudges, each with a gray V for wings.

"Where's the queen bee?"

Maya was impressed that Claire knew how bee colonies worked.

"Her name is Queen Bombadala," said Maya, and she drew a fatter smudge of yellow with a crimson crown.

"How come her crown is red?"

"Because it's made out of rose petal," Maya said

quickly. Claire's eyes were wide and delighted with Maya's answer.

"Tell me a story about Queen Bombadala."

"Well, once upon a time, when Bombadala was still a princess, there was an evil king named Darth Alcerius…"

Claire clutched Maya's arm and rested her curly dark head on her shoulder. Maya melted a little. She couldn't draw with Claire clinging to her left arm, so she put down the crayon and made up a long story about Queen Bombadala as a princess, searching for a magical rose that would defeat Darth Alcerius. The princess ran into various talking animals, and Maya did their voices, which made Claire laugh. The story was rambling and pointless, but Claire didn't seem to care. She listened until she dozed off.

"Rough afternoon, huh?" Seth asked when he came in and saw Maya, herself half asleep, with Claire snuggling next to her.

"Some of it was," Maya said honestly. "Then she conked out."

"Oh, I know all the little dramas." Seth crouched and stroked Claire's hair. "You can go now, if you can get out from under her."

Maya gently nudged Claire aside to free her arm. Claire's eyes popped open.

"I have to go potty!" she said.

* * *

Maya's afternoons with Claire grew easier as she got used to the little girl's mood swings. She found that most tantrums could be sidetracked with a new story about Princess Bombadala, who ended up foiling bank robbers, riding in the Kentucky Derby, and rescuing Claire's two dads from an army of man-eating broccoli. Sometimes she was helped by her brother, Rafael Basewalker. In the end, of course, the villains always turned out to be spies or assassins sent by the diabolical Alcerius.

Maya had never been so busy. She babysat two or three times a week and spent twenty minutes every morning in the garden, picking the unwanted grass and weeds that poked up through the mulch. She also had more homework as they neared the end of the school year. She read *The Miracle Worker,* identifying with Annie Sullivan as she weathered the tantrums of young Helen Keller. She wrote a paper on Dolores Huerta, picking her name off a list of famous Americans. She solved pages of math problems and tried to comprehend the scale of geological time.

The salvia bloomed first: little blue flowers popping up after a few weeks. Maya ran inside and made the family come out to see. Everyone was dressed and having breakfast. They gathered in the backyard, Dad still holding his coffee cup, Mom snapping a photo with her phone, Grace rolling her eyes.

"You plant stuff and it grows. What a miracle," she said dryly.

"It is!" Maya insisted.

"Let me get a picture of you next to the flowers," Mom said.

When she had time to herself and the computer, Maya searched for updates from the DR about Rafael Rosales. She also read Grace's blog. Her sister wrote updates practically every day. She'd deleted the past bits about Maya and didn't post anything new—nothing about Fledgling Fan, nothing about any kind of minor-league anything objects. They had an uneasy truce.

Sometimes Maya would finish her homework and come down to watch a few innings of a Twins game with Grace. She didn't ask questions or make comments, because Grace would roll her eyes and be annoyed. But she liked that time with her sister and liked watching the games. She even enjoyed the slow moments in the game as the pitcher shuffled around on the mound and the batter adjusted his gloves and looked into the dugout. (Why he did that, Maya didn't know—it was one of the things she was afraid to ask.) She got used to the rambling commentators, one apparently an ex-pitcher who favored loud ties, the other steeped in baseball knowledge.

It was the second announcer who mentioned Rafael Rosales one Friday evening in May. It was late in the game, and the Twins were trailing by six runs. Their turns at bat seemed quick and futile, and Grace had halfway stopped watching to study the Minnesota driver's manual.

"There's good news from the DSL Twins regarding prospect Rafael Rosales," said the announcer. Maya perked up and Grace set her manual down to pay attention, but the player batting for the Brewers hit a double and the announcer had to talk about that. It was a couple of batters later before he got back to it.

"You were going to tell us about Rafael Rosales," the ex-pitcher reminded him during a pitching change.

"Right! Rafael Rosales played very well in rookie ball and came to be ranked one of the top prospects in the organization. As a top prospect, he was invited to spring training, but he struggled. He had about six hits in eighty at bats and was let go before the end of the spring."

"But now, good news," said the ex-pitcher.

"Yep. Today the Dominican Summer League team kicked off their season, and Rosales went five for five with two doubles and an outright steal of home."

"Wow. You don't see that anymore."

"If you want to make a statement that you are still a top prospect, you do it like Rafael did today," the announcer said.

Maya felt a thrill. She wondered if there would be any video highlights on the Web, or at least a recap of the game. She realized her eyes were moist.

"Congratulations," said Grace, her voice only a little bit mocking.

CHAPTER 17

The Saturday before Memorial Day, Maya went out to plant forbs. She had a square plastic pot of thistle, which was prickly, and another of borage, which had fuzzy leaves and smelled of cucumbers.

She stopped and stared. There were three bees circling the tiny pink verbena blossoms. These bees were green instead of yellow, but their shape and sound was unmistakable. They looped and whorled around one another in what looked like a dance. She realized now she might get stung. The website said bees really didn't want to sting people, but that was easier to believe that when it was hypothetical. Now she had to grab a shovel and walk right among them!

She reminded herself that Rafael Rosales had stolen home base, an outright steal when the pitcher had the ball. She didn't know how a runner could surprise a pitcher that well, to slide across the plate before the ball got to the catcher for a tag. It was probably completely stupid, as Danny Rhombus would say, but that didn't matter. Rafael had gotten away with it.

She cautiously set a foot into the garden bed. A bee landed briefly on her shoulder, but she remained calm until it buzzed away.

* * *

"Your garden's looking really good," Grace told her later that day. She had just come back from a driving lesson and met Maya in the upstairs hallway.

"Thanks," said Maya. She was aching to tell someone about the bees, but wasn't sure Grace would appreciate it. "Uh…you're turning into a good driver." She had noticed that Grace now drove away a bit more smoothly, and that Dad returned from their outings a little less tense. "I'm sure you'll pass the test with no problem."

"Thanks."

They looked at each other for a while in the stretch of hallway between their rooms and the bathroom.

"Also, your Rafael had another good day," said Grace. "Three hits; one was a homer. He doesn't get a lot of those."

"He's not *my* Rafael," said Maya, although her heart soared. "But I'm glad he's doing well."

She got on the computer after dinner, navigated to a gardening discussion board, and thought about telling these people about her bees. They would get it and congratulate her. But she wasn't allowed to create accounts or post on the Internet unless Mom or Dad knew about it. She didn't want to test her luck.

Instead, she checked the minor league page for the DSL Twins. There was a box score but no recap. Stats instead of a story.

Finally, she checked Grace's blog.

"Our favorite player in the minors had a good game today," Grace had written in her post from the night before. "We'll keep an eye on him." Not a word about "Fledgling Fan," which left Maya feeling both relieved and disappointed. She felt oddly left out.

* * *

"I saw three bees in my garden," she told Claire the next time she babysat. "The first ones of the year."

"You said your garden was full of bees," said Claire.

"Those were invisible bees," said Maya. "These are visible bees."

"I want to go see!" said Claire.

"Me too," said Maya. "But we're not supposed to go anywhere."

"We can go to the playground," Claire reminded her.

That was true. Rodney had said so. And a trip to the playground would go faster than the usual two hours of floor puzzles and tantrums.

"Then let's go to the playground," she said. "It's such a nice day."

She found that getting out of the house wasn't easy. Claire wanted to bring a snack and a juice box, which Maya stuffed into a toddler-sized backpack. She also wanted Maya to pull her in the wagon, but before they left, she loaded the wagon with toys from a bin in the garage.

"I want to dig," she said, putting in a plastic bulldozer. "I want to swim and play ball." She added a pink pool noodle and a small beach ball with an octopus on it.

"You don't have a swimsuit on," Maya reminded her. Claire's face got a verge-of-tantrum look Maya had gotten to know too well. "But you can wade," she said quickly. "You can take off your Crocs and wade. It'll be fine." She would have to do the same thing, of course, but she didn't care if her legs got wet. "Are you going to ride in the wagon?" Maya wasn't sure Claire had left room for herself.

"Yes!" Claire climbed in, sitting on top of the toys. Maya hoped the girl wouldn't tumble out. She closed the garage door, pocketed the keys, and started pulling the wagon toward the park. Claire grabbed the pool noodle and pretended to row. It made the ride long and bumpy, and Maya had to retrieve the noodle whenever Claire dropped it, which was constantly.

"I have to go potty!" the little girl announced the moment they arrived at the park.

"Seriously?" Maya asked.

Claire's eyes were wide and urgent.

"All right, all right." Maya checked the bathroom doors on the side of the school, which were locked. She brought the wagon around the school's main entrance and found that door locked as well. She sighed. Did they have to lock up the moment school was out?

"I really have to go!" Claire said, clambering out of the wagon.

"I know," Maya said. "Listen, my house is closer than yours. We can go there. Get in the wagon and hold on tight."

Claire did, and Maya jogged, the wagon bouncing and rumbling behind her.

"Hurry up! I really have to go!"

"I know!" Claire called back.

Fortunately there was no traffic on Victory Memorial Drive, and she was able to drag the wagon across the street without stopping. She pulled the wagon into their driveway, and moments later Claire was in the downstairs bathroom. Accident avoided.

I should have reminded her to go before we left, Maya thought. An unpleasant, honest truth gnawed at her—she had slightly planned this stop, or at least knew it could happen. She knew her house was close to the park and that the school was often locked by four. She'd been a student there for six years, after all.

"I can't reach the sink!" said Claire.

Maya helped her wash up.

"Can we see your garden now?" Claire asked.

"Sure. But only for a moment."

"Will Queen Bombadala be there?"

"She's a very busy bee," said Maya. "But maybe." If they saw any bee at all, she could claim that was the queen and make Claire's day.

They left through the front door and walked around

to the back, Claire grabbing the pool noodle for no reason. She stopped when she saw the garden, her mouth dropping open. "Wow," she said.

The borage was now in full bloom, and there were too many bees to count. Maya couldn't believe her luck. Not luck, she reminded herself. Planning. These plants were supposed to attract bees. But it *was* amazing when things worked exactly the way they were supposed to.

"It's beautiful!" said Claire. "BEE-yootiful!"

"Ha," said Maya. "Thanks."

Claire swung the pool noodle through the air. She took a step closer and did it again.

"Don't do that near the garden," said Maya. "You don't want to hurt the plants."

"But one of the bees is bad!" Claire said.

"No. No. They're all good bees."

"It's a bad bee from Darth Alcerius!" Claire sliced the air again, this time sweeping the edge of the noodle through the prairie grass.

"No it's not," said Maya firmly. "Now knock it off!"

Claire kept at it, flattening some of the grass and looking like she might knock the blossoms off the borage. Maya swooped in, took the other end of the pool noodle, and stopped Claire from swinging it again. Claire made her mouth into a tiny O and let out a piercing, high-pitched shriek.

"Come on," said Maya. "All I did is stop you from wrecking my garden."

Claire still screamed, dropped her end of the noodle, and shoved her arm in Maya's face so she could see the angry red welt forming.

"The bad bee got me!"

"Oh, honey, I'm sorry."

"I told you it was bad," the girl said accusingly.

"Come on, let's go inside."

So they trooped back inside, this time through the back door, past her sister who was in the living room. "I'll explain later!" she said as she hurried Claire to the bathroom. She'd read about treating bee stings on one of the gardening forums. The most important thing was to get the stinger out as soon as possible.

Claire was crying, but at least she was still. She could have a total meltdown over getting a broken animal cracker, but in a real emergency, she was cool. Or maybe paralyzed with fear.

Maya sat her on the toilet and worried at the sting with tweezers until she extracted the slender hair-width stinger and dropped it into the trash. Claire winced when the sliver came out but was still quiet.

"We probably need to sterilize that," Maya said, taking a bottle of witch hazel from above the sink.

"It'll hurt!" Claire pulled back her arm.

"No, it doesn't. I promise. It's not alcohol." Claire let her splash the welt with the liquid. The sore spot looked puffier and redder than before, and Maya began to worry.

"Are you allergic to bee stings?"

"I don't know. I never been stung before." Claire's eyes were puffy now, and the lids looked heavy.

"Can you breathe OK?" Claire's breathing sounded rasping, but it was hard to know since she'd been crying.

"I can breathe," Claire said in a whisper. Now Maya was sure she looked puffy all over.

"Oh no," she said. "Grace!"

CHAPTER 18

Luckily, Dad had carpooled to work that day and the car was in the garage. Grace drove them to the emergency room at North Memorial Medical Center, her fingers white-knuckled on the steering wheel. Maya sat in back, holding Claire and making sure she was still drawing in air, which she did in thin, struggling gasps.

"I'm not supposed to be driving without a licensed driver in the car," said Grace. "Plus, it's against the law to have a child without a car seat." It had been her idea to drive the mile to the hospital instead of calling an ambulance, but now she was having second thoughts.

"It's an emergency!" Maya reminded her. "There's no way you'd get in trouble. Plus you're driving really good."

The cars behind them didn't agree, bleating their horns in frustration and zooming past them as soon as they got the chance. One guy shook his fist at them. Grace cringed and waved her hand in apology. She turned onto the road by the hospital and started to go the wrong way on the C-shaped driveway to drop off patients, but saw her mistake and steered away before an SUV came barreling down the driveway. More horns, more hand waves and rude gestures.

"Gee," she said. "You would think at a hospital people would be more understanding." She found the right turn and dropped them off at the entrance.

"I'll find a place to park."

"We need to call Rodney too," said Maya. She had the number memorized and recited it four or five times.

"All right. I have my phone." Grace drove away, leaving Maya to hurry Claire in the entrance. The girl was still breathing, but it sounded even more strained now. A woman in hospital garb saw them and whisked Claire and Maya away into a little room labeled Triage. Maya answered a barrage of questions from one nurse while another peered into Claire's eyes with a flashlight, checked her pulse, and tried to talk to her.

"So," the nurse said with a West African accent. "This child is having a severe allergic response to this insect sting. We must give her an immediate injection of epinephrine. Is her parent or legal guardian available?"

"No. I'm the babysitter. My sister is trying to get hold of her dad. One of her dads."

The nurses talked for two seconds and decided the injection was more important than protocol. Claire's eyes were too unfocused to notice the injector, and she barely responded when the nurse applied it to her thigh and held it in place for a few seconds. It looked more like a glue stick than a needle.

Claire's breathing was normal a few minutes later, but her eyes were still foggy. Maya moved a chair closer to her so Claire could lean against her shoulder.

"She is fortunate," said the nurse with the accent. "You got her here very quickly, and that was smart." Maya hoped Rodney and Seth would think so. It wasn't so smart to show a small child a garden full of bees. "Bee venom is not as strong in the spring," said the nurse. "It's worse in the summer, and then she might not be so lucky."

Maya swallowed hard. She had been gripped with fear for the past hour, but had not really believed—not deep down—that it was possible for a tiny insect to kill a person. What if this had happened later in the summer? What if Dad had driven to work and Grace didn't have the car?

Grace finally found them, her chest heaving because she'd been running.

"Both dads will be here soon," she said. "Is Claire all right?"

"She is now," said Maya. She wasn't sure that Claire would be all right, and the thought of facing Claire's parents filled Maya with cold terror. "We got her here in time."

Claire's eyes were now more alert. "I got a shot," she said, remembering what happened. "Do I get a lollipop?"

* * *

Rodney arrived short of breath and anxious. He nodded at Maya as he swept Claire into his arms and fussed over her.

"Thanks for waiting with her," he said. "Why don't you come by tomorrow and we can talk about what happened? I need to be all about Claire right now."

"Of course." Maya slipped out to the lobby. Grace was sitting there and playing on her phone.

"Claire is going to be fine," said Maya. She gave Grace a recap of everything that had happened in the triage room. "I guess we can go home."

"Dad's going to get us after work. His carpool driver will drop him off."

"Huh? Why does he have to drive?"

"Because it's not an emergency anymore," Grace explained. "I shouldn't drive without a license."

"Right." They could have walked home, but Dad would still have to come get the car.

Maya crossed the lobby and flipped through magazines in a rack. They were mostly news and celebrity gossip. She stopped at a sports magazine because the cover caught her eye.

THE CRADLE OF SUPERSTARS: SCOUTING BASE-
BALL TALENT IN THE DOMINICAN REPUBLIC

She grabbed it and paged through it until she found the cover story, starting on a two-page spread with a sepia-toned photograph of a pitcher in full windup.

For years, hot talent has been coming from this
small Caribbean country. Now it's coming at
top price. Find out why.

The chances of Rafael being in the story were close to nil, but reading it would pass the time. Maya returned to sit next to Grace, who saw the cover and gave her a thumbs-up sign. Maya had trouble concentrating on the story at first, but in a few minutes she was completely absorbed. Her father nudged her as she was reading the last paragraph.

"Let's go, hon. I guess you had a rough day."

Maya nodded, blinking back tears, and followed her father and sister to the car.

* * *

The next day was Saturday. Maya wheeled the wagon to Claire's house, not caring if she looked silly dragging a wagon full of toddler toys.

She thought about leaving it on the front path. She knew Rodney was expecting her to come in and talk, but now she was afraid to face him.

The door opened before she could make a decision. It was Rodney.

"Come on in, Maya," he said.

Maya sat in an armchair while the two dads sat on the couch, trading looks before they spoke. They'd obviously talked already about how to handle this. She'd never been in trouble with anyone besides her parents. This was a new feeling for her. Suddenly she was a problem to be solved.

Claire was napping, so everybody whispered.

"You've been really reliable, and Claire loves you,"

Seth started. Maya knew there was a "but" coming.

"And you handled the crisis yesterday really well," said Rodney. "You didn't take chances and got Claire to the ER, and we really appreciate that."

"I'm really sorry about what happened," said Maya.

"Anyway," said Rodney, "given that Claire had a scary experience, I'm going to cut back on my hours for a couple of weeks."

"And then it'll be summer," Seth said. "Claire is going into an all-day summer camp. So…"

"Am I fired?"

The two men looked at each other again, and Maya knew the answer.

"I wouldn't say fired," said Rodney. "But your services aren't needed anymore."

Maya's mom worked in human resources, so Maya knew that meant *fired*.

* * *

When she was back outside, Maya stared into the backyard at the plastic slide and turtle-shaped sandbox, feeling a pang of loss. It wasn't always fun to babysit, but it made her feel grown-up and important. She had also become fond of Claire, even with her prattling and mood swings.

When she got home, she walked around the house and into the garden. She saw that the door to the garage was open. It was probably Dad, tinkering with something.

She looked for bees in the garden but didn't see any.

She took a step closer and noticed something fuzzy lying in the grass. She stooped down and saw the tiny body of a bee. Was this the bad bee that had stung Claire? She knew bees died when they stung people. She picked it up gingerly, thought about burying it, and decided that was ridiculous. She carried its lifeless body to the garbage bins behind the detached garage, lifted the lid, and started to drop it in. There was a red canister in there, right on top of the pile. Something about it caught her eyes. She dropped the bee and removed the canister.

MAKE YOUR HOME AND GARDEN A NO-FLY-ZONE

KILLS OVER 200 INSECTS INCLUDING FLIES, WASPS, AND MOSQUITOES. WORKS FOR UP TO EIGHT WEEKS!

The Alceria logo was visible in the upper left. Maya's heart sank into her stomach.

She walked into the garage on legs that seemed to be made of jelly.

"What did you do?" she asked her father in a hoarse voice. He was kneeling by the mower, doing something with a wrench.

"Huh?"

"I found this." She held up the plastic canister.

"I sprayed your garden. Grace told me what happened, and I didn't want anyone else getting stung."

"The garden was for the bees!" Maya said weakly.

"Honey...what?"

"I planted that garden for pollinators, and this *kills* them," she said, tossing the container on the ground between them. "It says so right on the bottle."

"Most people don't want a bunch of bees in their yard," Dad said, confused.

Maya didn't have the energy to argue. She returned to the garden and started ripping up plants. The canister said the chemicals worked for eight weeks, which meant the treated flowers would go on killing bees—and butterflies and ladybugs—for months. The plants had to go. Her father started toward her, said something she didn't hear, then walked into the house, shaking his head.

The thistles tore her skin, and the milkweed wept on her hands. She couldn't rip up the grass, even wrapping it around her hand and pulling. The strands dug into her skin, but the grass didn't give. She got the shears from the garage and knelt down to do it, steadying the shears, which was hard to do with shaking hands.

In half an hour it was all gone, the hours and hours of work, the weeks of waiting were shoved into one of the heavy compostable bags. She rolled the top of the bag and left it by the recycling bin.

After showering off the dirt and chemicals, she closed the door to her room, lay on her grass-colored rug and looked at the sky-colored walls. This time it didn't soothe her. It was all so fake, she thought. Fake grass, fake sky, fake clouds, fake birds.

She tried to shut it all out by telling herself stories about Princess Bombadala, but when she remembered that she would no longer be able to tell those stories to Claire, a fresh wave of grief washed over her. Everything she had loved about her life was gone in one afternoon.

CHAPTER 19

Rafael, Eight Years Ago

"Do you ever want to be a pitcher?" Rafael asked Juan after school one afternoon. Over a year had passed since he started playing at the campo, and now another school year was underway. Rafael was in fifth grade. The days were long and stuffy, and Rafael got through them only by thinking about the hour or two of baseball he could squeeze in later.

"No." Juan glanced at his right hand. He still didn't have the large, strong palms and long fingers of his brother. "Pitchers only play once or twice a week. I want to play every day."

"Good point." Rafael hadn't thought about that. Watching most of the games from the bull pen would be boring.

"Plus the routine!" Juan added. "It's too much!

Hugo can barely use his arm the day after he pitches."

"It's that bad?"

"Even when he ices it right after, he has to rest it for a couple of days. That's how it is for pitchers. He's home today because it still hurts from Saturday."

"He was *estupendo*," said Rafael. Hugo had pitched against batter after batter as the boys tried to get a hit off him. Toward the end of the day it was a free for all, boys jumping off the fence to take a few swings, each wanting to see if they could show up the hot pitcher. Rafael had been thinking about it all day, fantasizing about standing as tall as Hugo had that afternoon. Hitters had big moments, but only a pitcher could be the center of attention for an entire game.

"What about you?" Juan asked. "Do you think about pitching?"

"No," Rafael said. Fantasies were one thing, but he had never liked pitching, not the way he loved to bat and run the bases. "I'm put on earth to punish pitchers."

"Matatán!" Juan laughed at his bravado.

"*Buenas tardes, muchachos!*" said a voice.

The boys looked up. A sandy-haired man was standing in front of them. "It was your brother who was pitching here Saturday the past, true?" His Spanish was heavily accented and clumsy. He was from the United States.

"Right," said Juan.

"His arm is still sore," Rafael added, wanting to cement his insider status.

"Of course," said the man. "He played very good. Tell him I'd like to talk to him." He offered a card to Rafael, who was closer, but Juan snatched it away.

"Thank you." The man nodded, and Juan strode away. Rafael had to hurry to catch up.

"What team is he from?" he asked.

Juan spun around.

"*Cierra tu boquete*!" he barked.

"What did I do?"

"You told a big league scout that my brother has a sore arm! Do you know nothing?"

"Sorry." Rafael still didn't understand. Maybe he did know nothing. "I'll shut my hole next time," he promised. Juan still glared at him. Rafael had never seen him this mad.

"I get it," said Rafael. "You're worried that if he knows…if he thinks that Hugo is hurt, he'll lose interest."

"There are one million boys the teams can choose from," said Juan. "A rumor is all it takes to ruin his future."

"Those million boys aren't Hugo," said Rafael.

"It's the truth," said Juan. "But we don't tell those men anything." He put a hand on Rafael's shoulder. "We'll all three be pros, but Hugo's the sure thing. When he gets signed, my family never needs to worry again. You know that."

"I know it."

"My mother won't sew T-shirts in that factory, and my dad won't crawl around in bathrooms."

"No," said Rafael. "Sorry. I was dumb as a stone."

"Next time be quiet as one," said Juan.

* * *

Rafael couldn't always play after school. When he went home to change his clothes, his father might ask him to help with chores or his mother would put him in charge of Iván. Rafael lived for Saturdays, when he could walk to the campo in the morning with Juan and Hugo, have lunch at their house, and run back to the campo again in the afternoon. His parents never pressured him to stay at home on Saturdays. They knew that day was sacred.

"You shouldn't keep eating their food," his mother fretted one evening.

"They barely notice," said Rafael. At the Santos

Garcia home, there were always guests on Saturdays: neighbors and friends and relatives Rafael could not keep track of.

"We should feed him then," she said. "Bring those boys here next week."

"What if Papa has his machines all over the table?" Rafael asked.

"It'll be on time. I'll talk to your father."

So Hugo and Juan ate at Rafael's house, amid the stack of broken appliances leaking loose wires. Papa had cleared off the table in plenty of time, as promised.

Mama and Papa ate without talking, but Juan asked a steady of stream of questions to fill the silence: How do you fix that? What did you put in the stew? His parents answered in two- and three-word sentences. Juan was on to the next question before they were finished anyway.

"Do you still like pirates?" he asked Iván.

"No," he said. "I learned in school that pirates are really bad people."

"Except for the Pittsburgh Pirates," Hugo joked.

The *sancocho* had pork sausage because there was company. Rafael fished more pieces out of the pot in the middle of the table before he finished the peas and rice on his plate. His mother saw him and scowled. He dropped the ladle. He felt suddenly like everything in his house was wrong. There was too much clutter and his parents didn't smile and there weren't enough people to create a clamor of conversation and there wasn't enough meat in the stew. He couldn't wait to finish and get out of there.

"Your friend Juan seems interested in my business," Papa said later, the dining room table once again sprawling with his repair work. "If he wants to learn, he can stay and watch. He can assist me when Iván isn't home."

"I'll ask him," said Rafael, knowing that he wouldn't, and that if he did, Juan wouldn't do it. Juan was no more interested in becoming a repairman than he was in becoming a housewife or the kind of pirate that did not play for Pittsburgh.

CHAPTER 20

One day, Rafael hit a home run, his first ever at the campo, off a fourteen-year-old pitcher named Bernardo. He usually swung for contact, to put the ball in play, to simply have a chance to make it to base. This time he swung the bat perfectly, and the ball seemed to fly and fly. Rafael was so stunned that he sat and watched it sail over the fence before trotting around the bases. The outfielder had to scramble over the fence to fetch it.

"Nice hitting," said a man behind the fence. "You have a good approach at the plate. Patient and disciplined." It wasn't uncommon for pedestrians to stop and watch for a few minutes, but this man had been lingering for a while and watching with more than casual interest. He was athletic and had nice clothes.

He might be a former player turned scout. Rafael's heart beat a little faster.

"Thank you!" he said. "I'm Rafael Rosales."

"Carlos Domingo." The man offered a hand, remembered the fence was between them, and settled for a wave. His hands looked strong, the kind that could crush yours if he wanted them to. "Pleased to meet you, Rafael. It's good to see young players who use their head. How old are you? Thirteen?"

"Twelve," said Rafael, rounding up.

"Really? You carry yourself like an older player."

"Are you with a team?" Rafael asked.

"No team," he said. "I'm a private coach."

So he was a *buscone*, a street agent. Rafael took a step backward. These men would help you train, maybe get you into an academy, but they would take a huge chunk of your future signing bonus.

"I'm not sure I want a private coach," he said.

"I'm not offering," said the man bluntly. "I've seen you hit one ball. That's not enough to go on. But I'll keep an eye on you. I am looking for a couple of boys with promise." He nodded toward the outfield. "I think they need you out there."

Rafael ran out to left field, hoping that the other

boys thought Carlos was a scout. They might say, "Big league teams are already talking to him," the way they did about Hugo.

His moment of glory didn't last long. The second batter hit the ball hard past the shortstop, straight toward him. Rafael stopped to let the ball come to him, the way he'd seen other boys do it, but the ball died before it rolled to him. Desperate to make up for his mistake, he lunged at the ball and booted it back toward the shortstop. He saw the pitcher smother his face with his battered glove as the player made it safely to third base.

Rafael scanned the smattering of people behind the fence, hoping Carlos Domingo was no longer watching. He sighed. The buscone was still there.

* * *

On the way home, Rafael waited for Juan to ask about the man he'd been talking to. He didn't, so Rafael had to explain ahead of the question.

"He was a buscone," he said. "Not a scout."

"Who was?"

"The man I was talking to."

"I didn't notice," said Juan. "But it's not a bad way to go."

"No?"

"My papa says ten years ago boys would try out for teams right off the street, but now they all come from the academies. And most of them have private coaches before that."

"*Por supuesto*," said Rafael, though he had truly never considered it. "Why don't you have a private coach? Or Hugo?" He felt a pang of guilt as he said Hugo's name. He still hadn't forgiven himself for mentioning Hugo's nagging injury in front of the scout they'd met.

"Maybe we will eventually," said Juan. "But Papa knows a lot, and he works with us both. See you tomorrow."

Of course. Rafael once again felt cheated by his papa, who didn't know anything about baseball and didn't seem to care if his son ever played in the big leagues.

* * *

"I met a private coach today," Rafael told his father that evening. It was that rare time in the day when neither of his parents was busy. Papa had pushed aside his repair jobs for the day and was relaxing in his favorite chair, chatting with Mama about a trip they had taken before Rafael was born. They both stopped when Rafael mentioned the coach. They looked at him blankly.

"He said I had patience and discipline," said Rafael. "He thought I was thirteen because of how I carried myself." His parents still didn't seem to understand. "Of all the boys there, he only talked to me."

Papa raised his eyebrows. "What was this man trying to sell you, and how much does he charge?"

"He's trying to sell me his coaching, and usually they charge part of your bonus, if and when you sign with a team. Otherwise they get nothing." Rafael wanted that to sink in. Somebody believed in him. Somebody had an eye on him anyway. "He said I have promise," he said, now stretching the truth.

"And if you fail, you become one of the *manganzones* who hang about the plazas, drinking beer and playing dominoes?" A manganzón was an adult that acted like a child. The word stung.

"No," said Rafael. "I would find a job."

"Doing what?"

For that, Rafael had no answer.

"Or worse," said his father. "Maybe you'll be like the boys who go to the United States and never return. They get cut by their teams and disappear."

"I would never do that," Rafael promised.

Mama looked back and forth from Rafael to Papa.

She looked like she might speak up, but didn't.

"This island has always been plundered by pirates," his father grumbled. "First they took the gold, then they took the sugar, then they took the beaches. Now they take our young men. They take and they take"— he shook his head—"and they throw things away when they're barely used."

* * *

"What'll you do if you don't ever get signed?" Rafael asked Juan the next day, as they walked home after school. He was still bristling from his father calling him a manganzón.

Juan laughed. "Live off Hugo!"

Rafael laughed too and wished he had a backup plan like that.

"It's him." Juan stopped, a hundred feet from his house. The sandy-haired American man they'd seen at the campo was at the house. He finished a brusque phone call, tucked the cell into his breast pocket, and tapped on the door. He was let in immediately.

"Isn't he a scout?" Rafael said in a whisper.

"No. I thought he was too, but he's an agent from an American company," said Juan. "His name is Peter White." He sat down on the curb. "He spent a long time talking to Papa and Hugo last night. He knows about Hugo's arm and still wants to sign him."

"I'm sorry I told him Hugo was hurt," said Rafael.

"He would know by now anyway," said Juan. "He brought a doctor over. They did a full exam. They're not going to sign a guy without an exam."

"Claro." Rafael had been brooding about it for days and now forgave himself.

Juan crept to the door, cracked it open, and listened for a moment. He shook his head, closed the door, and sat back down on the curb. "*Susurro, susurro, susurro,*" he said, mimicking the fervent whispers inside. "I can't hear a thing." Rafael sat next to him. There would be no baseball this afternoon, not with exciting things going on.

"Do you think Mr. White will want to sign you too?"

"No. I'm not Hugo," Juan said. "The US agents want the million-dollar contracts. I'll be lucky to sign for any amount of money."

"If you go to the United States and get cut from a minor league team, will you disappear?" Rafael asked.

"You remember my Yankees cap? From when we were little?"

"Of course."

"My uncle Miguel sent that to me. My father's little brother. That's what happened to him. He made it as far as Jupiter, Florida, but the Marlins cut him from their Class A-advanced team."

"Where'd he go?"

"He must have gone to New York, because he sent that cap."

"And that's where you would go?"

Juan pinched his lip as he thought it over.

"What would I do here? There's nothing." He shook his head. "I would find my uncle and live with him. What about you?"

"I don't have an uncle in New York," said Rafael. He would have to come home to face the shame of failure and his father's headshaking. And what would happen then?

CHAPTER 21

Maya

"Maya, wake up." Grace nudged her gently.

Maya peered at her sister through eyes gummy with sleep.

"It's summer vacation," she remembered. "Leave me alone." One thing she liked about her life these days was that she could sleep a lot. She turned over, but Grace shook her again.

"We have to go now," said Grace. "Get dressed."

"Go where?"

"You'll find out when we get there." Grace pulled the covers off Maya. "Bring your babysitting money. I'm broke."

Maya was more awake now. She sat up.

"What's going on?"

"It's a surprise. Meet me downstairs."

Grace was being annoying, but this was more exciting than another long day with nothing to do. Maya got dressed in her shorts and a T-shirt with an owl on it, dug her stack of twenties from her sock drawer—one for every time she babysat—and tiptoed downstairs carrying her sandals. Grace was waiting by the door.

"Can't we have breakfast first?" she asked.

"I don't want to wake Mom and Dad."

"Do they know we're leaving?"

"Don't worry. I left a note."

"Do you have dad's permission to use his car?"

"He's carpooling, and it's not his day to drive. It's Wednesday."

"But do you have permission?"

"I left a note!"

Moments later they were rolling quietly away in the Sonata, which Grace had left in the driveway the night before. She drove slowly, double- and triple-checking her blind spots for every turn and lane change. They ended up going south on Interstate 35. It was weird having Grace drive, but she seemed to know what she was doing. She'd gotten her license six days ago.

"Are we going to the Mall of America?" Maya asked.

"Nope."

"The big zoo?"

"How early do you think those things are open?"

"I don't know." Maya was already out of ideas. She watched the skyscrapers of Minneapolis get smaller and smaller in the rearview mirror. They were in far-flung suburbs before Grace took an exit, pulling into the parking lot of a McDonald's. It was probably the worst place on earth for the environment, but Maya was too hungry to care.

"I want to know where we're going," Maya said once they were in the booth.

"If you must know," said Grace around a mouthful of egg sandwich, "we're going to see the rabbits."

"What rabbits?" Maya asked.

Grace finished eating before she answered.

"*See* the rabbits. Come on, you can finish your sandwich in the car."

"There are rabbits in our own yard," Maya said as they crossed the parking lot.

Grace kept driving south. As they got farther from home, it felt more and more like they were fugitives. Maya half expected police to pull them over and tell them to go home. Maybe Grace would get arrested for stealing Dad's car.

"We should call Mom and Dad," Maya said. "Tell them where we are."

"I told you I left a note," said Grace.

"But they're probably worried about us."

"Well, I can't call because I'm on a provisional license," said Grace. "If I get caught using a cell while driving, I'd be in big trouble."

"I can call!"

"My phone is dead," said Grace. "I thought Dad's charging cable was in the car, but it's not."

"They have phones at rest stops," said Maya. "We could pull over."

"Maybe later," said Grace.

Maya dozed off, dreaming of bees and purple flowers. When she woke up, Grace was taking an exit into a small town.

"We need gas," she said. "You're paying." She turned into the lot of Casey's General Store and pulled up to a pump.

"Yay for me," Maya said flatly.

"It says to prepay inside." Grace got out and grabbed a nozzle.

Maya walked into the store and gave the clerk one of her twenty-dollar bills. She noticed a sign about not selling tobacco to minors, which told her she was in Iowa.

"Is there a rabbit show around here?" she asked the clerk.

"Not that I know of."

Maya felt ridiculous. "OK. Bye." She hurried out the door. Grace was done pumping gas and waiting in the driver's seat. Maya got in.

"We're in Iowa."

"I know." Grace pulled out of the parking lot and back onto the interstate.

"I still haven't seen any rabbits," said Maya.

"You will."

Grace took an exit and drove east past silos and red barns. Every time they passed a pasture of cows, they both called "Moooo!" because they'd done that since they were little. But there were more cornfields than cows. The corn was probably genetically modified and had neonicotinoids.

Maya was about to ask for lunch when they passed a sign for Cedar Rapids. She had a realization: around a mouthful of food, "We're going to Cedar Rapids" sounded like "We're going to see the rabbits."

"Why did you let me think we're going to see rabbits?"

"Because it was funny."

"What's in Cedar Rapids?"

"Stuff."

Five minutes later, Grace was parking in the lot of Perfect Game Field at Veterans Memorial Stadium, according to the sign.

"Baseball," said Maya. They'd driven half a day to see a game when there was a major league ballpark three miles from their house. "Why here?"

"Because minor league baseball is the best," said Grace.

"We could have seen the Saint Paul Saints," Maya said as they waited in line for tickets.

"Not the same thing," said Grace. "The Saints are not minor league; they're independent."

"Of course."

"It's worth the trip. You'll see."

Maya paid for hot dogs and sodas, and the girls found their seats behind third base. It was a pleasant day, sunny and not too hot, and Maya felt lazy and happy sitting in the bleachers and eating her hot dog. The announcer reeled off the names of the visiting Lansing Lugnuts. Then he started on the Cedar Rapids Kernels. Maya looked down at the row of players and felt her chest tighten.

"He's here?" she asked, turning to Grace. "Is that him?" She'd stopped paying attention to Rafael during her spell of hopelessness.

"He's here," Grace confirmed. "Your minor-league compassion object was called up."

CHAPTER 22

Rafael's first at bat came in the second inning. Maya thought he looked more confident than he had during spring training at Fort Myers, staring down the pitcher instead of scuffling around and looking over his shoulder. Maya stood up to cheer and Grace joined her.

"Down in front!" said a voice behind them.

"It's his first at bat as a Kernel!" Grace shouted back. "We need to make him feel welcome!"

Rafael bounced a base hit down the first-base line. He zipped all the way to third base before the right fielder ran down the ball and chucked it back into the infield. Now everybody stood and cheered.

"Triples are hot," said Grace.

At the end of the inning, a frizzy-haired woman with a camera came up the steps to their row.

"Hi, I'm Monica with the *Gazette*. I got a great picture of you two and want to use it in the paper, if you don't mind."

"I don't mind," said Grace. "Are you a sports photographer? How cool."

"I'm actually a reporter," she said. "I have to take a photo here and there too. It's a small paper."

"Oh. My. God." Grace got wide-eyed.

"She wants to be a sports reporter when she grows up," said Maya.

"And it's so cool to see a woman doing it," Grace added.

"It's pretty cool to *be* a woman doing it," said Monica. "Anyway, I'll need your names..."

After writing them down, she handed a card to Maya. "Email if you want a copy. And seriously, Grace, if you want to ask me anything about becoming a reporter, shoot me an email."

"I will. Thanks!"

The rest of the game was lopsided. The Kernels scored a bunch of runs. The Lugnuts scored a few but were way, way behind. In the eighth inning, Rafael sailed a ball over the fence, and the crowd stood and cheered. Grace looked at her smudged-up scorecard, and her eyes popped open.

"Rafael hit for the cycle."

"What's that?"

Grace pointed at the row on her scorecard representing Rafael's at bats. "He hit a single here, a double here, a triple in his first AB, and now a home run. That's the cycle. It's a big deal. As rare as pitching a no-hitter."

"Wow." Maya looked down and saw him by the home team's dugout, waving at the cheering fans. She was mostly happy, but she also felt an inexplicable twinge of loss. Now she had to share Rafael with all of Cedar Rapids. It was like the fox all over again: he didn't need her.

* * *

It wasn't even dark when they got home, but of course the days were long in the middle of June. Mom got to them first, hugging them both the moment they walked in the door. She squeezed them like they'd survived a fire. Dad loomed behind her, seeming twice as tall as he normally did.

"We're glad you're all right," he said. "But what you did was totally unacceptable. We thought about calling the police."

"We would have in another hour," said Mom.

"Maya shouldn't be in trouble," said Grace. "It was all my idea."

"I did have fun," said Maya. "I should be in trouble too."

"Don't listen to her," said Grace. "This is all on me."

"Did you have supper?" Mom asked Maya.

"Yes." They'd had personal-sized pizzas at the convenience store in Mason City.

"Then go to your room. We'll talk to you later."

Maya looked back at Grace, standing calm and blank-faced.

"Now," said Mom.

"Thanks," Maya mouthed at Grace.

***

Grace came up the stairs an hour later, her eyes red and watery. Maya met her in the hall.

"What happened?" Maya asked in a whisper.

"They said I behaved selfishly and irresponsibly. I can't use the computer or the car for a week."

"So you can't apply for any more jobs?"

"I already applied for fifty jobs," said Grace. "I don't care about driving, but the computer part is rough. I won't be able to blog. My readers will think I'm dead!"

"Do you want me to get on and tell them you're grounded?"

"Sure, but make it funny," said Grace. "Tell them I'm scouting baseball talent in Finland or something."

"Do they have baseball in Finland?"

"I don't think so. That's why it's funny."

"Will do," said Maya.

"Maybe not that," said Grace, "but something."

* * *

Maya logged into Grace's blog using the password she'd given her and found the new-post button. She stared at the screen, occasionally typing a line or two and deleting it. She tried to be clever like Grace, but her attempts fell flat. Then she did not try to write like Grace, and she didn't try to be funny. She simply told her story.

> Three months ago, I didn't care about baseball. Sports seemed like such a waste of time and money when the world has real problems. That changed when my family attended a spring training game and found out about a player named Rafael Rosales. He seemed like a nice guy, and when I found out he had the worst stats on the team, I started rooting for him.

She did not write about the garden. That was too hard, even now. She simply said that she was sad about something. She wrote about the trip to Cedar Rapids, her sister's mysteriousness, and the misunderstanding about rabbits. She wrote and wrote, trying to fix the misspellings that showed up with a red underline, but otherwise not worrying if it was any good. She wrote it the same way she used to narrate stories about Princess Bombadala to Claire.

> And so here is finally the point. Thinking Girl will be on a short time-out from the blog because she did a nice thing for me, something to give me hope and make me happy even though she knew it would get her in a load of trouble. She'll be back soon with the stats and sass we all love.

She titled it "We Go to See the Rabbits" and signed it at the bottom, Fledgling Fan.

She bumped the cursor over to the publish button but couldn't bring herself to do it. There was something wrong with the wall of text she was about to post. She clicked Save Draft instead.

It was late. Even Mom and Dad had gone to bed.

She remembered the card in her pocket. She took it out and sent a quick email to the reporter, asking for the picture of her and Grace. Monica replied with amazing speed, considering how late it was.

> Attached. Sorry, could not use the pic. Attribute if you use publicly.—M.

It was a beautiful picture. Monica had caught them both at a moment of surprised joy, celebrating the triple: Grace pumping both fists, Maya's own eyes wide and shining in the afternoon light. This was what the post needed. The photo was like an exclamation point on her post.

But would Grace like it? She'd never posted a photo of herself, and that was probably on purpose. Oh well, thought Maya. This couldn't be worse than driving to Iowa without permission. She figured out how to upload the photo, added a caption, and posted the blog entry. She read it once more, not quite believing she'd done it. Then, to stop herself from taking it down in a fit of second-guessing, she went to bed.

CHAPTER 23

"You blew up my blog!" Grace hollered from the office. She had jumped on the computer as soon as a week was up, exactly 168 hours after the punishment was handed down. Maya was lying on her rug, doodling bees and flowers in a notebook. She'd meant to write one of her stories, but the words weren't coming.

"Maya!" Grace called again. Maya dropped the pencil and ran into the office.

"I didn't delete anything." She looked over Grace's shoulder. "See, it's still there."

"I know, but look. I have almost seven hundred comments."

"What? There were none yesterday." Maya had even checked the blog a few times to see if anyone had responded, and no one had. She's been disappointed.

She'd hoped for at least some of the same friendly replies Grace always got.

"You didn't see any comments because they were held for moderation," said Grace. "But here they are, seven hundred comments waiting to be approved. And look at this." Grace opened a bar graph. The bars on the left were short; the ones on the right were tall. "This shows my daily hits. It used to be like twenty to thirty a day. Since your post, it's six or seven thousand a day. Not hundreds. Thousands. And—ahh! Look!"

She pointed at the screen like she'd seen a spider.

"What? I can't see because of your finger."

"This shows hits coming from *Sports Illustrated* and ESPN. Huge national websites are linking to my blog."

"Wow." Maya still wasn't sure if Grace was mad or excited. "That's good, right?"

"I don't know," said Grace. "I haven't even read your post. But whatever you did, it went viral."

"Viral?" Maya remembered a librarian trying to prove something about the Internet, posting a photo that made it to a dozen states and a few foreign countries in an hour. "Viral is bad, isn't it?"

"Sometimes," said Grace. "But not always. Let's see

what people are saying." She started scrolling through the comments.

"This is so sweet... 'Sharing with everybody I know...' 'This reminded me of the last game I saw with my ninety-year-old grandfather...' 'Fledgling Fan, you're lucky to have such an awesome sister.' At least one person is talking sense." Grace stopped. "I think that's enough to say it's the good kind of viral."

"I didn't mean to steal your thunder."

"*Pfft.* I didn't have any thunder."

"But you're a way better writer than I am," said Maya.

"I know," said Grace. "Well, I should read the post that gave the world chicken pox." She closed the comments box and started reading the post. Maya left the room, not wanting to hover. She couldn't stand to stare at a blank page anymore, so she resumed work on a jigsaw puzzle she'd started a long time ago: a nature scene with goldfinches perched on a pine branch. She'd gotten part of a branch finished when Grace yelled again.

"Maya, you better come in!"

Uh-oh. What happened? Was she in trouble? She walked back into the office.

"What?"

"We're invited to be on TV."

"Really?"

"If the offer is still good. It's from a couple of days ago. I missed it because of being grounded. Channel 5 invited us to be on the morning show. They would do a bit about how a girl blogger hit the big time. They mean you, but they want both of us."

The thought of having a camera pointed at her terrified Maya, but she had to do it. She'd blown up Grace's blog, and this might make up for it.

"Ask if they still want us," she said. "Hopefully it's not too late."

"Right." Grace started typing a response to the message. "I've still got hundreds of comments to read. It's killing me. I wonder how the big-time bloggers do it."

"Do you want help?" Maya offered.

"Sure, but not right now. If you're up before me in the morning, you can slog through and approve anything that isn't from a spammer or an obvious troll."

"What's a troll? Someone who wants to cause trouble?"

"It's OK if they disagree. Conversation is good for a blog. But if they are mean and pointless, delete. And if you're not sure, leave it for me."

"Will do."

Early the next day, Maya got on the computer. She first read Grace's new blog post ("I've discovered the secret to success: be gone"). That post had thirty or so comments, and there were a dozen new ones on Maya's post.

She read comment after comment, clicking the green check marks to approve them or the red X to delete. Most were kind, saying the post was nice, sweet, cute (she cringed), or "so adorbs" (she came close to deleting that one). She deleted a couple of mean ones and several spammy ones. She came to one that made her grit her teeth.

> Sorry, if women want to be taken seriously as sportswriters, they shouldn't talk about how cute the players are or play to cheap sentiment.

That wasn't fair. She had never used the word *cute*. She simply said that Rafael looked better clean-shaven. She saw that the comment came from Danny Diamond, with a link to his own blog. She deleted it with extreme prejudice. The link made it spam, right?

A few seconds later she came to one from a reader who called herself Jewel.

Hola from La Republica Dominicana! I find
this blog when I search news for stories about
Rafael. I have known him for years. Thank
you for kind words.

Of course the Internet was full of fakers and scam
artists. But if somebody wanted to trick her, they would
claim to be Rafael himself, right? Or they would ask for
money. Jewel said only that she knew him and didn't
ask for anything in return.

Maya opened an incognito browser tab, set up
a free email account, and composed a message to
Jewel.

Dear Jewel,
    Thank you very much for your comment
on the Thinking Girl blog. Sorry to ask, but
how can I know that you really know Rafael?
Leigh

She wasn't ready to sign her real name, so she used
her middle name. She fired off the message, then went
back to the blog and trashed the comment. For some
reason, she wanted this friend to be a secret. Grace had

a bunch of friends through her blog, and Maya just wanted this one.

* * *

She had a response later that day.

> Dear Leigh,
>
> My real name is Bijou, the word for jewel in my first language, Creole. I have always lived in the DR, but my parents are from Haiti. Here is a photo of me with Rafael from six years ago. This proves I know Rafael. Honestly! Rafael is in the background. The boy next to him is his best friend, Juan, and the boy showing me how to pitch is Juan's big brother. My father works for a baseball academy, and we both live here at the academy. So I know many baseball players, but to most of them I am nobody, a skinny Haitian girl in the hall. But Rafael always took the time to say hello when he was here.
>
> Bijou

The photo appeared as a thumbnail at the bottom of the message. Maya clicked to enlarge it. A boy was showing a girl how to hold a baseball while Rafael and another boy looked on. It sure looked like Rafael when he was twelve or thirteen. The boy with the baseball had a tight-lipped smile that looked forced. The girl was eight or nine. That made her fifteen now, since she said the photo was six years old. Maya was glad she was a kid.

Bijou,

My own real name is Maya.

Thank you so much for this picture. It is amazing to see Rafael as a boy!

I hope we can keep emailing. I have never had a pen pal.

Maya

CHAPTER 24

"So, I understand you two are Internet stars," Dad said at dinner. Maya nearly choked on a forkful of rice pilaf. Grace dropped her fork and put her hands on the table like she was trying to steady herself. "My colleague Meaghan saw the story on Facebook," he explained. "She said it had a lot of shares. Is that what it's called? A share?"

"Yeah," Grace confirmed. "Aren't you a computer nerd?"

"I never got into social networking," he said dismissively. "Meg showed me a screenshot. It said, 'This girl's blog will make you stop what you're doing and go to a baseball game.' And there was a picture of you two. Of course, I'm wondering when you started a blog"—Dad drew out the word—"and why my tween girl thought she should share personal information with the world."

"What personal information?" Maya protested. "I didn't even use our first names."

"It had your picture," he said. "It had your hometown."

"It said we were from the *Twin Cities*," Maya corrected. "We could be from Saint Paul or the suburbs…"

"Whoa. Hey. I'm not going to argue here," said Dad. "But it's startling to find out my daughters are famous on the Internet, when I don't even know they have a blog."

"It's *my* blog," said Grace. "I've had it for over a year. Maya wrote *one* post."

"Grace," Mom said in her that's-not-the-point voice.

"I've been careful," said Grace. "No real names, nothing specific about who we are, no photos."

"There *is* a photo," Mom reminded her.

"Maya posted that without my permission."

"And you didn't take it down?"

"It was too late," said Grace. "Besides, you see kids in the paper all the time. Four-year-olds feeding ice-cream cones to puppies. Do you think kidnappers see that and hunt the kids down?"

"Maybe!" said Mom.

"Then what's the big deal about a blog?" said Grace. "If we're in constant danger all the time, because terrible people lurk behind every bush and building..."

"Grace!" Dad interrupted. "You're getting carried away."

"Do I have to shut the blog down?" Grace asked, her eyes bulging, pupils darting between Mom and Dad, Mom and Dad, daring one of them to say it. They looked at each other. A long moment of silence passed.

"Seriously, all she writes about is baseball," Maya offered in a small voice. "It's not like she's having private chats with grody old guys or anything. It's fine."

"Sorry if we don't let our younger daughter decide what's best," Dad grumbled. "This is a grown-up discussion."

"You sprayed a *pollinator* garden with *insecticide*!" Maya said. "Shows how much you know. Being grown-up didn't help there!" She folded her arms and waited for him to respond.

Dad took a deep breath and exhaled slowly. Maya couldn't see his hand under the table, but she suspected he was taking five.

"I did," he admitted. "I acted hastily. And that's my

point. I didn't consider all the consequences, and that's why I made the wrong decision." Maya was too surprised to say anything. Was Dad kind of apologizing? "I know how much that garden meant to you, and it kills me every time I see the empty rectangle in the backyard."

"You could have told me that sooner." Maya wiped her eyes on the shoulder of her T-shirt.

"So, maybe you should have read more of my blog before you freaked out," Grace suggested timidly.

"If anyone told me what was going on in the first place, I might react better," Dad muttered.

Grace took a deep breath.

"Probably not the best time to bring this up, but I kind of need an answer fast."

Mom and Dad looked at her, puzzled.

"Can me and Maya be on TV?"

* * *

Dear Maya,

I looked up your phrase, pen pal, and I like the idea very much. I can practice writing in English and learn more about your life in the USA. What do you want to know about me? I have fifteen years. My favorite thing is domino, I think the word is the same in English? It is a fun game, and I am very good! It is very popular here, but sadly there are no million-dollar bonuses for playing domino. Tell me about you?

Bijou

* * *

Dear Bijou,

I am twelve and turn thirteen in November. I like to ride my bike, read, draw, and do jigsaw puzzles. I also like gardening. I had a garden this summer, but now it's gone. (It's a long and sad story.) We call the game dominoes. I don't know how to play, but I like most games.

Maya

* * *

Dear Maya,

You can tell me your long & sad story. I have time.

Bijou

CHAPTER 25

Rafael, Seven Years Ago

Every Saturday, Rafael waited for Hugo and Juan outside their house to walk with them to the campo. He was surprised one Saturday when their cousin came out first. He'd met Damian once before, when his whole family came from Yamasá to visit. He had four or five sisters that filled the Santos-Garcia house with squeals and giggles, the kind of happiness that rarely brightened Rafael's own home.

"I remember you," said Damian. "The boy with the fast bat."

"Sure," said Rafael. Had Juan described him like that? Had Hugo?

The brothers came out a moment later. Juan and Rafael sprinted ahead, excited to get to the baseball field.

"What's Damian doing here?" Rafael asked.

"He's turning sixteen next year and wants to try out for the big leagues. He's living with us so he can practice and be seen by scouts."

"Damian is a prospect?" The cousin had the same lanky build and big hands as Hugo, but his slouching posture and heavy-lidded eyes made him seem less than athletic.

"Sure," said Juan. "He plays all the time in Yamasá. He's good!"

"I didn't know that."

Hugo usually pitched on Saturdays, but he gave up his spot so Damian could show his stuff. It was also because of his sore arm, Rafael guessed, but he knew better than to ask. Hugo watched for a while but left early, a cloud of gloom almost visible over his head.

Damian didn't have Hugo's skill, but he could throw hard fastballs over the plate. There was something deceptive about his slow windup and delivery that caught batters by surprise. Rafael waited in the lineup for his chance to try to hit Damian's stuff, vowing not to let Damian trick him. When his turn came, he let two strikes go by, to time them, and fouled off two more before he sent one flying to the outfield. It missed being his second home run by inches, rattling off the fence and rolling back toward the infield. Rafael reached second base. He didn't come around to score, but his teammates all traded high fives and fist bumps at the end of the inning.

Rafael was playing third base that day for the first time. Boys called it "the hot corner," and he could see why. It seemed like two batters out of three hit the ball hard and in his direction, and if he wasn't careful, a line drive could take his head off. The danger made him hyperaware and alert. He felt like he was seeing with sharper eyes than he had since his first game at the campo. Late in the game, he leaped into the air and snared a ball. A boy on third was already breaking for home, and in two steps, Rafael touched the base. Two outs turned, all by himself. He was delirious with joy but played it cool, lobbing the ball back to the pitcher with a cursory nod.

I'm a third baseman.

Now he knew. He would have to play other positions, sure, but this was where he belonged.

"This boy owned me," Damian said as they left the campo, slapping Rafael's back. "Are you the next David Ortiz?"

Rafael laughed at the idea, comparing his slight build to that of the huge Red Sox hitter.

"Rafael!"

The boys stopped and turned around.

Carlos the buscone had been watching the game and now caught up with them.

"I saw how you studied the pitcher the way good hitters do. Excellent fielding too. I continue to be impressed by your maturity. And only twelve. Hard to believe."

"Thank you," said Rafael. "This is Juan. He's good too!"

"I've seen you play," said Carlos, his voice conveying no opinion about Juan's ability. "I know your brother is an up-and-comer. Is this him?" He looked at Damian. "You do look like the Hugo I've heard of. And you pitched...well."

Not well enough to be Hugo, Rafael knew. But he also knew better than to blurt out that this wasn't Hugo, because that might give away that Hugo was hurting.

"I'm a bit rusty," said Damian, not confirming that he was Hugo but not denying it.

"Well, Señor Rosales, I'd like to talk to you further,"

said Carlos, turning back to Rafael. "With your parents present, if this is something you would like to pursue. I can give them references. People who will vouch for me, players I've worked with…"

As he went on, Juan and Damian started again for home, probably not wanting to intrude. Rafael tried to listen, to remember everything Carlos told him. There would be a formal tryout, the chance to see Carlos's home, which had a small gym and practice field. Rafael and his parents could talk to three different boys in academies now, all who would tell him Carlos had helped them get there. Rafael's head was spinning. Somebody really believed he had a chance. Somebody who seemed to know about baseball.

"All right," the buscone said at last, handing him a business card. "Talk to you soon, Rafi." Nobody called him that except family, but Rafael didn't mind.

"*Muy bien*," he said. "My papa will call." He fought the urge to put in another plug for Juan, but it would have to wait. He hurried to catch up with his friends.

"Matatán!" said Juan. If he was jealous, he didn't show it.

* * *

Rafael waited until that quiet spell in the evening

when nobody was busy. He dropped the card on his father's lap.

"This man wants to talk to you."

"Is he your private coach?"

"Sí."

"I don't know anything about him," said Papa. "How am I supposed to trust him with my son's future?"

"He said he can provide references. Names of boys he's helped get into academies."

"Academies?" Papa echoed. "What do these academies do? Take you out of school?"

"I still have to go to school," said Rafael. Through eighth grade, anyway, he didn't add. That seemed like forever: the rest of this year and two more—he wasn't sure how he would ever make it.

"It doesn't hurt to talk to him," Mama said, at last speaking up.

"It doesn't hurt," Papa grumbled. "We don't always know the hurt of things." He left the card on the table next to his chair. "It's too late to call now, but maybe tomorrow."

But Papa had still not called a few days later, and Rafael began to worry. He even avoided the campo the next day because he did not want to see Carlos

Domingo. He did not want to explain why his father hadn't called. Maybe Carlos would think he wasn't serious. But a week later, he got home from school and found Carlos Domingo sitting at the table across from his father, a stack of papers in front of him.

CHAPTER 26

Rafael's father signed the papers a week later. They promised Carlos thirty percent of Rafael's future signing bonus. In return, Carlos would train him and help him find a spot on a team. Carlos could quit on Rafael at any time, for any reason. But if Rafael quit, his father would owe Carlos salary and expenses for the training he'd done. His father emphasized the last bit: if Rafael quit, his father would have to pay Carlos for his time and equipment. That would be quite a lot of money, more than they could afford.

"I won't quit," Rafael promised. He did not sign the contract himself, but he swore the next four years of his life against the fate of his family.

"Now, I need to see his birth certificate," said Carlos. Rafael nearly stopped breathing when his father pushed a folder across to Carlos. The buscone raised one eyebrow as he saw the date on his birth certificate.

"You're eleven?" His voice was stern. "You told me twelve."

"I rounded up," said Rafael. From the look on Carlos's face, he felt a sudden panic that the whole arrangement was about to fall apart.

"You can never lie to me again about anything. Even if it feels small to you."

"No," said Rafael. He felt it wasn't enough. "No, Señor Domingo."

"Call me Carlos," he said. "But always tell me the truth."

* * *

Carlos lived in a nice part of town, in a house with a wall around it and an iron gate. The house had a gym and a practice yard, a batting cage and tees.

"Did you buy this with your signing bonus?" Rafael asked, wide-eyed, the first time he saw it.

"No, the bonuses weren't as big back then," Carlos explained.

"Did you play in the big leagues?"

"Almost," said Carlos. "Made it as far as double A and was set for triple A the next year, but I played winter ball for the Licey Tigers and got hurt."

"I'm sorry," said Rafael.

"It wasn't even an on-field accident," said Carlos. "A scooter hit me when I was crossing the street." He shook his head at his own bad luck.

None of that answered Rafael's question. How did Carlos pay for this house and all the equipment?

"I had a backer," Carlos told him, guessing at Rafael's thoughts. "One of my best friends from the Wichita Wranglers is with the Royals now, making millions a year. I talked him into investing some of his big-league money down here in the DR. I'll pay him back when I get a few players signed."

"Is he Dominican?"

"No. He hasn't even seen this place," said Carlos.

Rafael's debt went deeper than he thought. He owed Carlos, and in turn Carlos owed this player in Kansas City. Rafael was burning with curiosity to know who it was, but if Carlos wanted him to know, he would have told him.

The first week of training, he swung a bat without even using a ball. One day, he didn't even use a *bat*. Carlos had him put his hands on his waist and pivot, trying to keep his balance as his weight shifted. Hitting practice was mixed up with fielding drills and mini-lectures about game situations and how to play each batter. It was a lot harder and a lot less fun than Rafael had thought it would be, but he saw the difference when he played at the campo on Saturdays. He hit the balls straighter and farther than he ever had before. He made better decisions in the field.

Carlos drove him home in the evenings and sometimes came in and talked to Papa. They would drink Clamato and talk about Rafael: how he was doing, what he needed to work on. But the conversation would slide as easily into politics, history, machinery, and other subjects. They seemed to share all the same interests and have all the same opinions.

They agreed that the Dominican Republic needed more financial independence from the United States and Mexico, and were horrified by how the government was treating displaced Haitians. They agreed that history cast a long shadow over the country. Strangely, given Carlos's career, they rarely talked about sports. But one day they wandered onto that topic.

"I've always wondered how things work," Carlos told Rafael's father, staring at the repair projects lined along the wall.

"It comes natural to me," Papa said. "I might have

been an electrical engineer if I'd gone to college."

"Why didn't you?"

"I wasted those years trying to be a fighter." Papa raised a fist like he was fending off a punch. "I was good, but I quit when I found out he was on the way." He gestured at Rafael.

"Good thing," said Carlos. "You still have your brains."

"And my hands," his father said. "Have you ever seen the hands of an old boxer?"

"I've seen the hands of old catchers," said Carlos. "It's not pretty."

Rafael had heard his father talk about fighting from time to time, but didn't know he'd been a *boxer*. He'd always imagined Papa was talking about street scuffles—and exaggerating at that.

"Did you dream about being a famous boxer?" he asked after Carlos had left. Papa was still at the table, nursing the dregs of his Clamato, which he drank without mixing in beer or rum as other men did.

"Every night for most of my boyhood," he admitted.

"Do you ever wish you hadn't quit?"

"No," he said. "I wish I'd quit it sooner, so I could be more than a repairman now."

Rafael searched his father's face for signs of regret for the boxing career that never happened and couldn't find them. He was telling the truth. He could live without his sport, but Rafael thought he could never live without baseball.

CHAPTER 27

"Any news?" Rafael asked Juan one Friday morning, the moment Juan slipped out the front door.

"Not yet," said Juan.

They were on a weeklong break from school, and Hugo and Damian had been visiting major league academies in Boca Chica, Guerra, and El Toro. Hugo had his heart set on one of the sprawling, modern major league academies in one of the smaller towns between San Pedro and Santo Domingo. Damian was hoping to get signed straight onto a team.

"They probably don't offer right away," said Rafael. "On Monday, they'll all start calling. Your dad will have to change his number, it'll be ringing so much."

"Sí. Hugo is the real deal."

Damian came out of the house, good humored and

relaxed as always. For ten minutes he told stories about the tryouts: the former pro pitcher who was now too fat to reach past his own gut, and the big Jamaican player who could knock the stitches out of a baseball but didn't know the rules of the game. He did impressions that made Juan howl with laughter. Rafael couldn't set his own nervousness aside to laugh. What would happen to Hugo? Why wouldn't the academies invite Hugo on the spot? If you didn't get into any academy, your baseball career was over before it began.

Rafael would have hung out with Juan longer, but it was getting late.

"I have to go see Carlos," he said. The buscone was running double drills during the break so Rafael could spend more time on school when it resumed. He would have given anything to stay, waiting with Damian and Juan to learn Hugo's fate.

"Go, Matatán," said Juan. "You're my backup plan now."

* * *

Carlos still wanted Rafael to play at the campo on Saturday mornings. The practice was important, he said. Rafael would always stop at Juan's house so they could walk over together. He knocked on the door the next morning and Hugo answered, bleary-eyed and wearing only shorts.

"Juan says he's tired," he said. "We all stayed up late, waiting for a call that never came. Maybe he'll play after lunch."

"I can't play this afternoon," said Rafael. "I'll see him at school."

The following week, Juan himself answered. He told Rafael he didn't feel like playing.

"Are you going to play ball ever again?" Rafael asked. "All the boys ask about you."

"Maybe next week," said Juan.

But he didn't come out that Saturday either, and Rafael didn't knock. He waited, tossing a stone high into the air and catching it on the way down. He thought of the game they'd played as boys, seeing who could hit a sock ball the highest. Back then, he felt like his whole future depended on Juan. Maybe Juan's now depended on him? He tossed the stone in the air ten times, then ten more times, and ten more.

He quit waiting and walked to the campo, arriving before the teams were decided and the game underway. He knew how Juan must feel. Hugo had given all of his boyhood and his right arm to this game, but the game owed him nothing back. Rafael had no way to help Hugo, to give him the health and fat contract he deserved, but he had to help Juan.

*　*　*

He brought it up with Carlos that evening, after a grueling drill in the batting cage.

"You said once you were looking for a *couple* of boys with promise," he said. "Maybe the other boy can be my friend Juan."

"I've watched him play," said Carlos. "He might have more muscles than you, but he doesn't have your determination. He's a poor risk. Probably a waste of my time."

"He's not a waste of time," said Rafael.

"I can put muscles on a boy and teach him the game," said Carlos. "I look for seriousness, maturity, and discipline. Those are things I can't teach."

"But Juan..." Rafael started to protest, but what could he say? Juan hadn't even played in weeks. When he talked about his own future, it seemed like he had already given up. "But Juan makes me play better."

"You're a good friend," said Carlos. "He can come and work out with you, but he's not my project or my problem. If he makes any trouble or distracts you, he has to go."

"Thank you!" said Rafael. It was a thread of hope. If Juan could come and show Carlos how serious he could be, maybe Carlos would coach him. Of course, he'd have to convince Juan to be serious, but he could do that.

He was so excited that he had Carlos drop him off at Juan's house and banged on the door as Carlos dove away.

"Carlos said you can—" Rafael started to tell him, but he stopped when he saw who was in the house. Hugo, Juan, and their father were there, of course, and so was the sandy-haired US agent. But Rogério Romero was there too. The famous Rogério Romero! He was now retired from the Dodgers but still had the glow of royalty.

"Sorry, I didn't know you had company," Rafael said in an awed whisper.

Juan stepped outside and softly shut the door.

"Rogério is opening an academy for pitchers," he explained. "He's going to help Hugo."

"Wow." Rafael felt staggered. A few minutes ago, he'd felt self-important to be inviting Juan to train with an ex-double-A player. Now Carlos's credentials seemed like nothing. But that was *Hugo*. He had always been special.

"I have good news too," he said. "Carlos said you can come practice with me, and if you show some intensity, maybe he'll take you on too." Carlos hadn't said so, but Rafael was sure it was true.

"I can't," Juan said. "I'm also going to Rogério's academy. He's going to teach me how to pitch."

CHAPTER 28

Romero's academy opened that summer, housed in a concrete building that used to be a shoe factory. It had an expansive courtyard almost the size of an infield. There were four boys at first: Hugo and Juan, Bernardo, and a boy from Santiago named Felipe. Felipe could throw a ball eighty miles an hour, Juan said, but his aim was so poor that he couldn't hit the ocean from the beach. Carlos had nice facilities, but Romero's were better. Besides the field, there was an expansive weight room, four bull pens, a swimming pool, and a sauna. The campus also had a dining room and a dormitory with eight beds, though so far only Felipe needed a place to sleep.

Romero owned the place, but he didn't run it. For that, he hired an old Cuban pitcher named Señor

Cádiz, who dressed like a caballero and squinted at the world through a cloud of cigar smoke. There were other coaches and trainers who worked part time, but Cádiz was always there.

Rafael often spent the mornings in the gym at Romero's academy. Cádiz didn't allow guests, but he made an exception for Rafael once he learned he was working with Carlos. "You must be a good one," he'd said. "Carlos can see through a wall of *mierda* a meter thick."

"Cádiz doesn't like me," Juan grumbled one afternoon.

"Sure he likes you," said Rafael.

"He hardly spends any time coaching me," said Juan.

"It's because you're younger than the others," Rafael suggested. "You have more time."

"No, it's because he thinks I'm a waste of time."

"Did he say that?"

"Practically. He said he's not seeing progress."

"Ouch. Does he know you're used to playing in the outfield?"

"Of course he does. Come on, let's lift before the older boys get here."

"Sure."

Rafael did several slow, steady bench presses of half his weight, with Juan spotting him. When it was Juan's turn, he slid on extra weights and lifted in quick bursts, grunting with effort.

"Carlos told me to do your reps slowly and extend your arms all the way," said Rafael. "That way you don't lose flexibility."

"But this is how to pump up and look good for the girls!" Juan finished his reps, sat up, and admired himself in the full-length mirror on the wall. He had packed on muscles since he'd started at the academy.

"Do you want to look good for girls or for major league scouts?" asked Rafael.

"For girls, of course. What about you?"

"I'll look good to girls when my pockets are full of money!" said Rafael.

"Matatán!" said Juan.

Rafael laughed. He only acted that way around Juan, who would never be fooled.

Hugo came in, looking dead serious. He chose a couple of light hand weights to do curls. Felipe came in a few minutes later but leaned against the wall instead of working out.

"Still rehabbing your throwing arm?" he asked Hugo.

"Cádiz wants me to take it very slow and easy," said Hugo. "I'll be fine."

"With me, it's the opposite. I must have thrown two hundred pitches yesterday."

Juan now finished another round of lifts, so vigorously that he was sweating. He admired himself in the mirror some more. Hugo hurled a towel his way.

"Wipe your sweat off the bench, Señor Musculoso."

"This towel smells like it hasn't been washed since Cádiz used it as a diaper," Juan complained.

"This place is filthy," Felipe agreed. "Pigs would have moved out by now."

"And all he ever has for lunch are tortillas and cold meat from the colmado," Hugo added. "Cádiz knows a lot about baseball, but he needs a woman to cook and clean for us."

"You *machistas* need to clean up after yourselves!" Cádiz barked, coming into the room. "I'm your coach, not your mother."

"Tell Romero to part with some of those millions of US dollars," said Juan. "We can have a maid each and a full-time cook."

"He hasn't earned one peso off any of you," Cádiz reminded him. "And he won't until one of you gets a big league contract. I'd like to see the mansion you lived in before, so now you can demand a maid apiece. I'd like to hear more about the seven-course meals you're used to eating."

"I was kidding about that," said Juan sullenly.

"We don't need a maid each, but we can't do laundry and cook while we're training," said Hugo.

Cádiz nodded. "I'll see what I can do about getting help."

* * *

Carlos was now coaching a second boy named Javier. He was from San Pedro too, but far enough away that Rafael had never seen him at the campo. He was a year younger than Rafael and a head taller. He was so tall and skinny he reminded Rafael of the sugarcane that grew on the farm where his father used to work.

"Did you see my swing?" Javier asked after batting off a tee, hammering balls in the cage on the small field near Carlos's home. "Did you see how I scooped up that ball?" he asked during fielding drills.

"Sure," Rafael said. "You're doing great."

Javier always passed on Carlos's offer of a ride home.

"I like the walk," he said.

"You should come to my house," he said to Rafael one day when they were done training. "We can practice some more."

Rafael was exhausted but didn't want to be shown up by Javier, so he accepted the invitation. The walk wasn't far and was back toward Rafael's own neighborhood.

They did not practice so much as talk about their futures while lobbing an old ball back and forth in the street near Javier's house. Javier talked, almost to himself, about his elaborate plans for the United States. He would hire a filmmaker to make a movie about his own rise through to the majors. He would marry a Spanish-speaking American girl to translate for him. He wanted to play for the Marlins because he had family in Miami. He'd planned it all out. Rafael knew that Javier wasn't all talk. He was eager to learn and seemed to remember everything he'd been told once.

If a team had one more spot on signing day, and it was between him and Javier, Rafael wasn't sure who would get it. In fact, he couldn't think why they'd want him, since he was a bit older and a bit smaller than Javier. However, he chose not to worry. Five hundred players were signed every year in the Dominican Republic, so there was room for both of them when the time came.

CHAPTER 29

Maya

Grace and Maya signed in at the front desk of the TV station and were sent to the green room, which wasn't green at all. Maybe it had been green once, and the staff never got out of the habit of calling it that. There were a couch and a few chairs, a refrigerator stocked with bottled water, and a wide-screen TV now showing the morning news. Maya was wearing the skirt and sweater Mom had bought for school picture day. They were too warm for the weather, but the studio was so over-air-conditioned that Maya hugged herself.

Mom and Dad had wanted to come, but Grace had begged them not to.

"I don't want to be seen as a kid," she'd said. "Besides, you'll make me more nervous."

Maya agreed. This felt like something they needed

to do alone, like the road trip and blog post that led up to it.

Grace looked at the bulletin board covered with signed photographs of people who had been through the studio. She tapped one of a very young Prince, the most famous person who ever came from Minneapolis.

"Wonder how much this would get on eBay?"

"Nineteen ninety-nine," Maya suggested.

"More than that—" Grace started, until she got the joke. "Good one," she said.

Maya sat down and felt the butterflies swirling in her stomach. She tried to visualize herself being calm and clear-spoken. Other guests came into the room: a tall leather-jacketed woman with a guitar; a gray-haired man who tried to make small talk with the musician; another man carrying a big box.

"Chef," he explained.

"Music," said the woman, holding up her guitar case. "Like you couldn't guess."

"Children's book author and illustrator," said the gray-haired man. "Patty the Pigeon?" He looked hopefully at Maya because she was the youngest one in the room.

"Oh yeah!" she said with faked recognition.

"You're the kids with the blog," said the chef.

"It's my blog," said Grace.

"Are you nervous?" he asked.

"They don't look nervous," said the musician. "They're a couple of cucumbers." Maya liked her.

They were on after the chef, who showed the shiny-haired woman how to make a perfect omelet. Maya and Grace talked to Colin, the super-smiley blond guy, in the fake living room set. He laughed long and hard when Grace said she didn't know for a week that her blog was an Internet sensation because she was grounded.

"So how do things go viral?" he asked. "For example, there are billions of cat photos on the Internet, and then Grumpy Cat becomes as famous as Elvis. How does that happen?"

Grace shrugged. "If anybody knew, everybody would do it."

"And why Rafael Rosales?" he said. "Of all the minor leaguers out there, why is he your favorite?"

"Maya better answer that," said Grace, giving her a nudge. Besides smiling and saying "Hi," she hadn't said one word so far.

"He was nice to my sister," she said, barely getting her voice above a whisper. "And I felt sorry for him."

The host laughed again.

"That's my baby sister," said Grace. "Lost kittens and slumping baseball players..."

"And bees," said Maya.

"Excuse me?" The host leaned in to hear her better.

Maya found her voice and told him about the bees.

* * *

"Well, I guess we don't have to be worried about getting invited back," Grace said as they drove home.

"Nope," said Maya. "Sorry." She hadn't planned on talking about bees, but what was the point of being on TV if you couldn't talk about what mattered?

Grace took a long, scenic route home instead of the highway, along the same streets where Maya rode her bike.

"Dad is going to be so ticked off," she said. "You went off on his company."

"Colin asked what was killing the bees, and I told him," said Maya. "I had to answer the question." It had been a couple of minutes before the host realized the segment had lurched away from "cute kids who blog" to a frank discussion of impending environmental doom.

"The neonicotinoids are meant to make the crops pest-resistant, but they also affect beneficial insects,"

Maya had explained. The words had come to her easily, even the big ones. "You can't poison the leaves without poisoning the pollen. Companies like Alceria invested a lot of money in making the neonicotinoids and deny their impact because it would be...well, because it would cost a lot of money to stop making them." She'd almost forgotten where she was, until she noticed the anchor staring at her, blank-faced and slack-jawed.

"Bees, baseball..." Colin had stammered, trying to find a path back to the lighthearted segment he'd expected. Maya felt bad and tried to help. "It's scary to be a kid right now, but Rafael Rosales gives me hope!" she'd said quickly. "That's all." The segment ended, and Colin left the set shaking his head and muttering. The shiny-haired woman swept them away.

"That was *interesting*," she'd said. She was using the Minnesota meaning of "interesting," which was "bad, but I'm too polite to say so." Cora the musician had been off to the side, playing her guitar between segments. When Maya glanced at her, Cora pumped her fist.

"Dad is going to be so ticked off," said Grace again.

"I know," said Maya. Until Dad came home, at least, she could savor that fist pump and feel like a troublemaker instead of a kid in trouble.

She jumped on the computer as soon as they were home, knowing Grace would hog it most of the day and she might be banned from screens after Dad got home. She was happy to see an email from Bijou until she read it.

Dear Maya,

Wow, you made more money babysitting than my father makes working. More in a week, not even the same number of hours.

Back in Haiti, there is much poverty and no work. Here in La Republica Dominicana there is also poverty, but some work at least. Before the academy, my father never had a job for long & we traveled a lot. Haitians are not loved here.

Things are better now. I went to school and even learned English. But we are still not wanted by most people.

I am sad about your bees and don't want to make you feel bad. Life is different for me, that is all. I wanted to tell you my own sad story. Thank you for sharing yours.

Bijou

Maya felt short of breath. Even though Bijou had ended her email on a nice note, Maya sensed that her new friend was upset with her. Well, Maya was privileged and she knew it. She didn't know why she had mentioned how much she made babysitting. She couldn't seem to open her mouth these days without hurting somebody.

She wrote a quick reply:

> Sorry, Bijou! I didn't mean to brag. And you can tell me anything anytime. It didn't make me feel bad.

The last part wasn't completely true, but she didn't want Bijou to think she had any hard feelings. She hoped Bijou would write back immediately to say "Of course I'm not mad" or maybe even "I'm sorry." Maya paged back through the earlier emails and looked again at the photo of Rafael as a boy. He was standing in the background while the older boy with the tight-lipped smile posed with Bijou. She studied the shadows in Bijou's face and tried to guess at the hardships in that little girl's life.

"Haitians are not loved here," she had written. What secrets lurked behind that simple sentence?

Maya clicked to write another reply and typed:

I don't understand, but I want to.

After she sent it, she felt like she was trying too hard.

Bijou did not write back.

CHAPTER 30

Dad came into the house with heavy footsteps and no words, the way he did when he was in a bad mood. He hung up his keys on the hook by the door and took off his shoes with brusque movements. Maya was waiting at the kitchen table. She knew she owed him an explanation and had spent time preparing herself.

"How was work?" she asked, just to break the silence and get it over with.

"I saw your interview," he said. His eyes met hers. "I watched it with my whole work group, including my supervisor." The last two words hung heavily in the air.

"Oh," said Maya. She had thought about Dad getting mad at her, but not about her dad's boss getting mad at him. "Are you in trouble?"

"I don't know." He shook his head and opened the fridge for ice water, taking forever to fill the glass. "I don't think I can get fired for something my daughter said on television," he said after taking a drink, "but I'm not looking forward to the next staff meeting."

"I didn't say anything that wasn't true," said Maya.

"You said things that haven't been proven."

"Yes they have," said Maya. "An entomologist at the University of Minnesota says..."

"You mean that Jenkins woman," her father said dismissively.

"Yes," she said. Maya was surprised her dad knew who Dr. Jenkins was. But of course he did. Dr. Jenkins must be public enemy number one at Alceria.

"We're not the big, evil company she says we are," he said. "Yes, we want to make a profit. But we also feed millions of people. *Millions.* To do that, we need to protect crops from pests. And we developed neonicotinoids to *help* the environment. That way, farmers don't have to drench everything in chemicals."

"But the insecticides kill the good bugs too," Maya argued.

"We did our own studies," he said. "They were inconclusive."

"And tobacco companies do studies that show cigarettes don't cause cancer," said Maya. She'd prepared the comeback in advance, knowing what Dad would say.

"I work for Alceria. I think I know more about what's going on with our products."

"Dr. Jenkins is a *scientist*. She knows what's going on with bees."

"I'm a scientist! Agriculture is an applied science!" He dropped his empty glass in the sink with a clatter.

"But you're not a bee scientist!"

He stood there, speechless for a moment. Maya realized she'd actually won the argument. Dad had no comeback.

"You put me in an awkward position at work," he said.

"I didn't mean to," Maya said meekly. "I didn't even plan on talking about the bees, but it kind of came out. I sure didn't know you'd be watching it with your boss."

"Well, what's done is done." He held his arms out, and she stepped into his hug. She still loved him even if he was working for a big, evil bee-killing corporation.

"Am I grounded?"

"No, I don't think that would teach the right lesson,"

her father said. "I want you to feel safe speaking your mind. But, you know...think about everybody that it affects. And make sure you know the whole truth."

Like Alceria thinks about everybody they affect, Maya thought, but she swallowed the words because she didn't want to argue anymore.

* * *

Dad was quiet at dinner, shoveling food into his mouth without making eye contact and chewing every bite too long.

"I put gas in the car," Grace said. "I refilled the windshield washer fluid."

"Good," said Dad.

Grace gave up on sparking conversation, pushed her plate away, and left the table. Dad soon left himself, marching through the family room and out the back door. Maya was left alone with her mother, who was done eating but lingering.

"He's super mad at me," Maya said.

"I think he felt a little blindsided," said Mom. She put her hand on Maya's. "We both love you."

"I know."

Maya heard the lawn mower starting up outside. The lawn did not need mowing.

There was still no reply from Bijou the next morning. Maya started another email of her own, apologizing more profusely, but deleted it. She didn't want to seem too desperate.

She went to the garage and unlocked her bicycle. Last summer, her parents had decided she was old enough to go on rides alone, as long as she stuck to the paths, wore a helmet, and was careful at the few busy intersections. But last summer she had been slightly afraid to do so.

Today she took the bike to the bike path and headed south, out of the neighborhood. She rode past the hospital and memories of Claire, past the golf course where Dad once gave her putting lessons, past the lake where she learned how to swim so many years ago. She entered new neighborhoods, stretches of the city where she'd never been before or done anything. The path wound around the lakes of south Minneapolis and eventually crossed the river into Saint Paul, but Maya stopped there at the river, in sight of Fort Snelling.

I did that all by myself, she thought. She turned the bike around and rode home.

* * *

"We can watch the Kernels tonight, if you want," Grace

told her when she walked into the kitchen, tired and sweaty.

"Is it on the Web or something?"

"Yeah. It's the free webcast of the day."

"That would be cool," said Maya. She got a glass and filled it with cold water.

"I called Mom, and she says we can watch it while we eat dinner," said Grace. Their mother usually didn't allow any screens during mealtime. She said it was family time and would even kick Dad off his laptop or make him put his phone away. "She said we can hook up Dad's laptop to the TV."

"Wow." Maya downed the glass and poured another. Had water always been this good?

"She thinks we need a family night," said Grace. "I think she means she wants to look at something besides Dad scowling."

"I know I do," said Maya.

* * *

There was still no email from Bijou. Maya stared again at the photograph of Bijou and the boys. She had already tried to imagine Bijou's life before this photo was taken. Now she wondered about the boys. They were baseball players now with big bonuses. What had their lives been like before they signed? The boy with the tight-lipped smile seem to have a lot of worries for a boy his age.

* * *

Maya made dinner herself, sizzling hot dogs in a pan, mixing up a bag of coleslaw with dressing, and popping corn in tribute to the Kernels. She took time to be grateful for all of it: the food, the nice stove, the family she would eat with. She found some of Dad's favorite beer in the pantry and made sure one was cold.

Dad seemed slightly confused by the whole thing, but he let Grace hook up the laptop to the TV. He settled into the armchair, took a long drink from the beer, and put his feet on the ottoman.

"I'm not going to lie to you," he told Maya. "This hits the spot." He set the bottle on the end table and scooped up a handful of popcorn.

"Kind of a no-frills broadcast," said Grace. She and Mom and Maya shared the couch. The view of the field was limited to one camera behind the backstop, and instead of live commentary, the video piped noise from the stadium.

"I like it," said Dad. "It's more like being at the game."

"Is that the guy you like?" Mom asked Maya as

the pitcher for the Wisconsin Timber Rattlers took the mound. The camera zoomed in on him as he threw his warm-up pitches.

"Wrong position," Grace teased. "Wrong team."

"Sorry, I thought it was him."

He didn't look like Rafael to Maya, but he did look familiar.

"Did we see this guy in spring training?"

"Nope," said Grace. "This team is affiliated with the Brewers, not the Phillies. But you probably saw his face on the Internet somewhere. He's a great big deal."

That magazine article! Maya remembered. She'd read it in the hospital lobby on the day Claire was hurt. His name was Juan something. He had two last names. But he looked even more familiar than a photo she'd seen once. She couldn't figure out why.

The game was in Appleton, so the crowd roared with every strike as their great-big-deal pitcher got quick outs. He cruised through the first inning, but in the second inning, Rafael walloped a ball over the outfield wall. Maya clapped in excitement. It was his second home run as a Kernel, and she'd seen them both.

"He's still hot," said Grace.

The camera showed the pitcher getting a new ball

from the umpire as Rafael circled the bases. The mike picked up groans and boos from the crowd.

The next time Rafael batted, the pitcher threw an inside pitch that grazed his jersey. Rafael took a step toward the pitcher, pointing and shouting something the mike didn't pick up. A couple of teammates quickly stepped in. Rafael was ushered to first base while the Rattlers pitcher kicked around on the mound.

"Message pitch," said Grace.

"That could have hurt him!" Maya protested. This big-deal pitcher was a jerk.

"It's part of the game," said Grace.

Maya didn't want to give in that easily.

"I don't think trying to hit people on purpose is 'part of the game.'"

"Yeah, but you're too perfect for this world," said Grace. "I'm going to go see how the Twins are doing." She stalked up the stairs. Dad glanced at both of them but didn't intervene. He probably agreed with Grace, thought Maya.

The Rattlers won the game in ten innings. By that time, Mom was putting dishes away and Dad had dozed off. Rafael had played well, but images of the standoff between him and the pitcher stuck in Maya's head.

Grace had gone to bed, so Maya got on the computer and checked her secret email account. There was still no email from Bijou. That was when a realization hit Maya like a bolt of lightning. The tight-lipped boy showing Bijou how to grip a ball...*that was Juan Whozit-Whatshisname on the Rattlers.* She found the web page for the Wisconsin Timber Rattlers and looked at his profile page. Juan Santos Garcia. Age: 20. Birthplace: San Pedro de Macorís, Dominican Republic. Sure enough, he was from the same hometown as Rafael and about the same age, though he looked older than Rafael in that photo.

But Bijou's email said the boy standing next to Rafael was Juan, and the other boy was Juan's big brother. The brothers looked a little alike, but Maya was sure the older boy with the baseball was the Rattlers pitcher. He had the same worried look as the pitcher. He also had the same broad palms and long fingers, and hands that looked a size too large for his body. The boy who was supposed to be Juan had an easy smile and ordinary hands. Of course boys grew and their bodies changed, but large hands didn't seem like something you'd wake up with one day, like a pimple or leg hairs. They would have always been big for his body.

Dear Bijou,

Are you sure the boy showing you how to pitch isn't Juan? I saw him pitch today (on TV) and...well, I wonder if he and Rafael are still friends.

She explained a little about what happened. She added at the end:

And about that other thing, please forgive me and write back.
Maya

* * *

The days crawled by. Maya went for bike rides in the morning when it was cool and spent the afternoons in her room. Sometimes she listened to the Kernels games over the Internet, the audio feed halting and several seconds behind the action. She would see the score update on the website before she heard the play announced.

Rafael's batting average dropped. As he struggled, Maya listened to the games even more fanatically, whispering encouragement when he came to the plate. Her long-distance pleading didn't seem to help.

Grace got a job at Dairy Queen, which was good

news except that they expected her to work the Fourth of July weekend. Mom and Dad didn't want to leave her alone for the week or split the family in half, so they called off their traditional week on Lake Mille Lacs. Maya had been really looking forward to the trip.

Bijou still didn't write back.

CHAPTER 31

Rafael, Six Years Ago

Rogério Romero wanted more students at his pitching academy, and because he had a famous name, he didn't need to comb the streets. He put up a sign that the academy would have open tryouts for boys aged twelve to fourteen on a Monday morning a few weeks into summer vacation. Rafael came that day to find the line of hopefuls wrapped around the corner and down the street. He thought he might have to wait in line simply to get in and watch, but Juan and Hugo arrived and ushered him inside. They blew past the line of boys feeling like royalty.

"Lot of competition," said Rafael.

"Might not be room for me when they're done," said Juan.

"Of course there will be," said Hugo. "You're crucial."

"Sure I am."

Señor Cádiz readied a pitch speed gun and had Bernardo and Felipe each throw a few pitches into the practice net. They both threw pitches around seventy miles per hour, which was respectable for their age. Rafael was still getting used to distances measured in feet and speed measured in miles per hour. The academy used the same measurements as major league baseball.

Hugo waited his turn, but Cádiz patted his shoulder.

"Better save your arm."

"What about me?" Juan asked.

"Sure, throw away." Cádiz handed him the ball but didn't stay to watch. He handed the gun to Bernardo and headed for the equipment room with one of the assistant coaches.

"Go," said Bernardo.

Juan hurled the ball with all his might; the speed gun said forty miles per hour.

"You're getting there," said Hugo.

"I would be better if I had any actual coaching," Juan grumbled.

They all took a turn except Hugo. Rafael even had a go and got the same as Juan: forty miles per hour.

"I'm lucky today," he said.

"I'd like to see that *Cubano* pitch," said Juan. "I bet he can't even get a ball to the net."

Cádiz was back with a bag of balls and had heard every word. He dropped the bag, took out a ball, and whipped it into the net, hitting the red target area smack-dab in the middle.

"Ninety-one!" Bernardo announced, looking at the pitch speed gun.

"Wow," said Felipe. "That pitch had more smoke than his fart-smelling cigars."

"I'm still good for one of those a month," Cádiz said with a sly smile. "Now I have to go ice my arm."

"So he can pitch," Juan grumbled after Cádiz was gone. "Too bad he can't teach."

"Give him time," said Rafael.

Romero finally arrived in a Cadillac SUV, the line of boys standing back in awe as a real major leaguer walked by. He was followed by a man with a camera who snapped photos as Romero came into the practice field, shouting hellos to the boys and the coaches. He took Hugo by his non-pitching arm and led him to the pitching rubber on the practice field to give him a lesson he didn't need. The cameraman snapped a million photos.

"I'm surprised he didn't bring a TV crew," Rafael whispered.

"Are you still mad about the last time?" Juan teased.

"Last time?" Felipe asked.

Juan told him through gasps of laughter about the time Romero had shown up in his and Rafael's neighborhood.

"He wanted so bad to be in the picture," said Juan. "He would have followed Romero home like a little dog."

Rafael got him back by telling Felipe about the Dodgers cap. "Juan wore it every day for years, and I'll bet he wore it at night," he said. "He wore it until his big head split it open."

Both boys laughed themselves hoarse. Rafael heard a snicker and turned to see that a skinny girl had quietly appeared behind them. As he'd promised, Cádiz had hired a cook and housekeeper, a tall, muscular Haitian man named Martin. The girl was Martin's daughter, and Cádiz had cleared a room for them to live at the academy. Rafael had never spoken to the girl, but he often saw her watching him on his visits. The boys sometimes teased him, calling her his girlfriend.

"Hi!" he said. The girl became shy and looked down.

"Let's get that girl into the picture!" Rogério Romero beckoned to the Haitian girl. He didn't ask who she was or why she was there. She timidly stepped forward. Romero crouched beside her, pretending to show her how to hold a two-seam fastball.

"And now one with both of you," he said, nudging Hugo back into the frame and handing him the baseball. "This'll be great for the brochure."

"Does the academy take girls?" one of the onlookers called.

"If they can pitch. Why not?" Romero stepped out of the frame. The girl timidly took the ball, barely able to grip it with her small hands. Hugo crouched and helped her. The cameraman snapped a picture.

"That's going to be a good one," he said.

Rafael saw the girl once more as he was leaving.

"Hi," he tried again.

"You caught a chicken for me once," she said.

"What? A chicken?" It took him a moment to remember: that day at the batey, the hen fluttering by him and Iván. He had caught the chicken like he was fielding a wicked grounder.

"How did you recognize me?" he asked her.

"I wasn't sure at first. I asked the boys if your father

ever worked at a sugarcane farm. Juan told me he did. My name is Bijou."

"My brother still talks about you sometimes," said Rafael. In truth, Iván hadn't mentioned her in at least a year, but for a long time he returned again and again to the little Haitian girl and her chicken. Rafael couldn't wait to tell him he'd seen her. "I can't believe it's you," he said. "It's a small world."

"It's a big world," said Bijou with a serious look. "But it's a small city."

* * *

Rafael was late getting to Carlos's house, and Carlos was unimpressed when he explained that he'd stopped at Romero's academy to see the tryouts.

"You're my student, not Rogério Romero's," he said.

"I know. Sorry."

"Your partner was left waiting," he said, gesturing at Javier, who was taking half swings with a bat. It was something they were practicing—holding up when they realized a ball wasn't hittable.

"Sorry," Rafael said again.

"Never mind," said Carlos. "Let's go hit some balls." They drove out to an abandoned field to the north of San Pedro, as they did on days when Carlos wanted them to practice hitting. It was the site of another closed sugar farm, but not the one where his father used to work.

Rafael was off his game that day, and having Javier encourage him made things worse.

"Good form," Javier said when Rafael whiffed on a lazy curveball Carlos had pitched to him. "Nice try," he shouted later when Rafael chased after a fly ball and missed the catch by six inches.

At the end of the day, they hammered ball after ball deep into the field, the two boys vying for distance. Javier seemed to hit farther, his bat flicking out with lightning speed.

"Go out and fetch the balls," said Carlos when they'd exhausted their supply of baseballs. "Whoever gets the most can ride back in front." He handed them each a canvas bag.

Javier whooped and ran out to search for the old balls. Rafael ran languidly after him, not caring if he was in the front of the old truck. But as Javier started to find balls and stuff them into his bag, Rafael felt like it was more than a made-up game to make them hurry. He put on a burst of speed and started snatching baseballs from the grass, his eyes searching for the muddy white against the washed-out yellow. Most of the balls were scuffed up, a few bursting at the seams.

When they returned, out of breath, Javier was laughing. Carlos dumped both bags on the ground and counted. Rafael had collected seventeen balls; Javier, fourteen.

"There's one more out there," said Carlos. "I had thirty-two."

"I'll find it!" Javier sprinted off. Rafael took one step, but Carlos stopped him.

"Might as well let him go. You already won your place up front."

"Thanks."

"So, any contenders at the academy this morning?"

"Nobody as good as Hugo," Rafael said honestly. But the tryouts had reminded him of how many boys in San Pedro could play baseball. They had all grown up with bats in their hand, it seemed, or hurling balls made of socks against concrete walls. They all had dreams of the big leagues, and not everyone would make it.

CHAPTER 32

Maya

Grace poked her head into Maya's room the Monday after the Fourth. She was in her DQ cap and polo shirt. "I have to go to work. You're home alone for a couple of hours."

"I'll protect the house if robbers come." Maya was lying in bed, reading a teen novel she'd checked out from the library. It had a bee on the cover but wasn't as much about bees as she'd hoped.

"Hey, if you get a chance," said Grace, "I have a blog post drafted. Can you read it? If you don't like it, I won't post it, but…"

"Why do you want me to read it?" Maya interrupted. "Is it about me?" What could Grace even say about her? Maya hadn't done anything interesting lately.

"It's not about you," said Grace. "It's about Rafael."

Maya groaned. There was nothing nice Grace could say about Rafael these days.

"If you think it's not too mean, go ahead and post it," said Grace. "I'm still logged in."

"OK."

"Bye!" Grace ran down the stairs.

"Thanks for asking me!" Maya said, too late for Grace to hear.

* * *

By now, you all know Rafael Rosales, the unofficial official Twins prospect of Thinking Girl's Baseball Blog. But you've probably also noticed that TG has recently fallen silent on Rafael news, and that's because, well, because TG is Thumper at heart: she'd rather say something nice or nothin' at all. But people keep asking, so here goes:

Rafael's bat is colder than Minneapolis in January.

Rafael is slumping like a rag doll left out in the rain.

Rafael has regressed so fast he's left a crater in the mean.

You get the point.

His batting average is now .239, which doesn't look that bad, but not so long ago it was 390. Not so long ago, his fellow Kernels didn't want to sit next to him on the bus for fear of popping. But now he'd make an ice-cream cone want to put on a sweater.

Rafael can't go back to rookie ball at this point. The Twins signed ten prospects in the international draft, and they are now swamping the roster in the DSL. Rafael has nowhere to go except up, or out of baseball forever. His June swoon came late and better end soon.

Maya sighed. It was a funny post, but she felt so bad for Rafael that she couldn't laugh. She posted it, then opened an incognito window on the web browser and logged into her private email account.

Dear Bijou,

I wish we were still pen pals.

I am worried about Rafael.

PLEASE WRITE BACK. At least let me know you're OK.

Maya

She included the link to Grace's blog entry and sent it, then watched YouTube videos of cats for twenty minutes to pass the time.

She checked her email again. There was no reply. Bijou probably wasn't online.

She heard a car door swinging shut and Dad shouting, "Is anyone home?" She put the computer to sleep and drifted downstairs.

"How was work?"

"You know," he said.

She didn't, but decided not to press him.

* * *

The next morning she finally had an email from Bijou.

Dear Maya,

Sorry I didn't write back sooner. It wasn't fair of me.

I read your sister's article about Rafael. I did not understand all of it (rag doll? crater? popping kernels?) but I get the idea. Rafael has always been up and down, up and down. More up than down. Does it make sense in English to say he thinks too much? I would say don't worry, but in truth I worry too. I also think too much.

Bijou

Maya wrote back immediately.

Bijou,

I am so glad to hear from you. If there were prizes for thinking too much, I would have a room full of trophies! I think too much about melting glaciers and acid in the oceans and bees. I even think too much about thinking too much. So I will continue to worry about Rafael.

When he does well, Rafael gives me hope. Now that he is failing, I feel like we're all doomed. It's like the fate of the world depends on how he does. Do you think I'm silly? My father would call it magical thinking.

Your friend,

Maya

* * *

Dear Maya,

I am not superstitious, but I like your type of magic.

Also, I am happy to be called your friend.

Your friend in return,

Bijou

* * *

She emailed Bijou a lot over the next few days, especially in the evenings while listening to Kernels games on the Internet. Maya wrote about school, family, and being on TV. As she wrote the last one, she thought she might seem spoiled and privileged again, so she added:

> Don't think all American children are on TV all the time. It was dumb luck, and I messed it up anyway.

But Bijou wasn't offended.

> Oh, I never want to be on TV. I want to be RICH, not famous! ;-)
>
> But do you know Rafael was almost on TV one time? I mean as a child. He is on TV all the time as a player. There was a big baseball star giving baseball lessons in the street. Rafael wanted so bad to be seen with

the famous player, but he wasn't picked. Instead it was his best friend, Juan. Rafael was mad with jealousy.

Juan! That reminded her. Maya saw the green light next to Bijou's name and clicked on it to open a chat window.

Maya: Hi!

Bijou: My typing in English will be slow.

Maya: I don't mind. I have a dumb question.

Bijou: ???

Maya: Remember that picture you sent with Rafael as a boy?

Bijou: Yes of course.

Maya: You made a mistake, I think. The boy with the baseball looks like the man I saw on TV. I emailed about it earlier.

Bijou answered surprisingly fast.

Bijou: Sure. You're right. That is Juan. I don't know how I made that mistake.

Maya: I knew it.

Bijou: U should be a detective.

Maya: :-)

Maya: Next I will investigate how to stop Rafael's slump. :-(

Bijou: Good luck.

CHAPTER 33

Maya took her bike out the next day. It was hot, even in the morning, so she stopped at the golf course and turned around. As she rode back, she heard a familiar voice.

"Maya!"

She squelched to a stop. There was Claire, wrapped in a towel and riding home in her wagon with Rodney pulling. Claire leaped out and ran toward her. Maya got off the bike to give her a hug. Rodney looked both confused and embarrassed.

"Maya!" he said.

"What happened to day camp?"

"Oh, that didn't last a week!" he said. He mouthed: "Biting."

"Oh no! Claire, you didn't."

"I wanted to use the swing, and another girl was on

it," Claire explained.

"No teeth. Never use teeth unless you're arguing with a carrot!"

Claire squealed with laughter. "I want Maya to come home with us!" she said.

"Not today," said Rodney. He looked at Maya. "Unless you want lunch?"

* * *

Maya dried and dressed Claire while Rodney made sandwiches. Claire took two bites of her crust-off PB&J, then clambered out of her high chair and staggered over to the couch to lie down and sleep.

"She's so tired," said Rodney. "I couldn't get her out of the kiddie pool." He set his turkey and Swiss back on the plate and wiped his hands on a napkin. "So how's your garden?"

"Not good." She explained what happened.

"Oh, I'm so sorry. Seth and I wanted to do a pollinator garden, but now that we know about her allergies"—he shook his head—"obviously we can't."

"Do you still have your job?" Maya asked.

"No. I'm a stay-at-home dad again, since day camp didn't work out. What have you been doing?"

Maya told him about her blog post. He must have

been one of the six people in the world who hadn't read it. They finished their sandwiches, Rodney occasionally glancing over at Claire.

"You know, she misses you," he said.

"I miss her too," said Maya.

"Maybe you can babysit again."

"I'd love to."

"I'll talk to Seth," Rodney promised.

Claire still wasn't awake after lunch. After an hour, Maya put her bike helmet on and got ready to leave.

"She's going to be upset when she wakes up and you're gone," Rodney whispered.

"Tell her I'll come back this weekend and play," said Maya. "I'll tell her a story."

"It seems like you've grown a lot in the last two months."

"I don't think so," said Maya. "My clothes still fit."

"I don't mean taller," he said. "I mean older. When I saw you on your bike, at first I thought you were Grace."

Maya laughed. "I don't think I'll ever look like Grace." They looked sort of alike, but Grace was... Grace was Grace. Even when she was Maya's age, she was bigger and sturdier than Maya was now.

She had a thought riding home. Would Rodney mistake her for Grace if the two of them were together? No, because putting them side by side highlighted their differences. If someone was looking through old pictures, they might mistake Grace for Maya or Maya for Grace, but there's no way they'd be confused if they were both in the photo.

And there was no way Bijou would make that mistake with Juan and his brother.

A new idea emerged. What if Bijou had not made a mistake? What if she was telling the truth the first time and was lying now?

There was only one reason she would do that.

***

Maya found Grace in their shared office space.

"Blogging about last night's Twins game?" Maya asked.

"Yeah," Grace said. "Hard to sustain enthusiasm the way they've been playing, but I want to be professional about it. Analyzing all their flaws is a lot of work! What's up?"

"I'm wondering…would a baseball player lie about who he was?"

"Huh?"

"Like, play under a different name. Pretend to be someone else."

Grace turned around in the chair to face her.

"Tony Oliva used his brother's passport when he came to the United States so scouts would think he was younger. I heard about it once on a Twins broadcast."

"Why would he do that?"

"He thought he had a better chance of being signed. Teams want to sign younger players. They have more time to develop and more years left in them."

"That was a long time ago though, right?"

"Yep," said Grace. "But that still happens, especially with foreign players. Are you worried that Rafael isn't Rafael?"

"No, I'm sure Rafael is Rafael," said Maya. "I was wondering for no reason."

"Sure you were," said Grace suspiciously, but she spun back around to work on her blog.

When Grace was off the computer, Maya spent an hour doing Web searches, looking futilely for photos or information about Juan Santos Garcia. There were too many useless links to sort through—stories from the last few years about Juan's multimillion-dollar signing and speculation about when he would ascend to the majors.

But when she started typing "Dominican players lying…" it auto-filled to "Dominican players lying about age." There were a half-million results. Apparently it was a big problem. It was especially common for players to use a brother's birth certificate.

She cleared the browser history so Grace wouldn't see what she'd been doing. If she saw the search results for Juan Santos Garcia along with baseball players lying about their age, she'd put two and two together.

What if the man playing as Juan really was Juan's big brother? That would be a multimillion-dollar swindle. Maya didn't even want to know if it was true. If it was, and she knew about it, she might have to do something about it.

CHAPTER 34

"Tomorrow is Bring Your Daughters to Work Day," Dad said that night at dinner.

"That's in April," said Mom. "And it's not called that anymore."

"Fine," he said. "It's Bring *My* Daughters to Work Day. I thought I would take the girls so they can appreciate what I do." He put special weight on the word *appreciate*. He picked up his turkey burger and took a big bite.

"Do I have to go?" asked Grace.

"Yes," he said firmly.

"But Maya is the one who talked smack about your company on TV!"

"You're acting like it's a punishment," said Dad. "It's not. I haven't had you to the office in a while, and tomorrow is the perfect day for it. I have plenty of time to show you around in the morning, and there's a presentation in the afternoon you might like."

Grace mimed a wide yawn. Dad pretended he didn't see it.

"You know," said Mom, "it's not too early for either of you to start thinking about your future."

"My future is not working at Alceria," said Maya, picking at her carrots.

"Do you think when I was twelve I planned on being a market analyst in agribusiness?" asked Dad.

"Of course not," said Maya. But she had a hard time seeing him doing anything that didn't involve spreadsheets. "What did you want to do?"

"I wanted to study outer space. Maybe even travel to other planets." His eyes got a faraway look. Maya found space travel a million times more interesting than his real job.

"That would be so cool," she said.

"It would," Grace agreed.

"It's a nice idea, but if I were on my way to Saturn, I wouldn't be here for you girls."

"What about you, Mom?" Maya asked. "What did you want to be when you were a kid?"

"I sure didn't plan on going into human resources," said Mom. "But the position of Patrick Swayze's wife was taken."

"You didn't have bigger dreams than being some guy's wife?"

"Well, I was sort of kidding, but—" She thought hard. "You know, this is what I wanted. This family."

"Being some guy's wife!" Maya repeated. She couldn't believe it. Her dad dreamed about exploring space, and her mother dreamed about having a family?

"When you get older, you might appreciate it," said her mother.

"I do now," Maya said. She didn't want to hurt her mother's feelings or ruin the first nice family conversation they'd had in days. But she wanted something more than a house and kids.

"I'm going to be a sports reporter," Grace said, filling the awkward silence. "It's not a dream. That makes it sound so pie-in-the-sky. It's a plan."

"You already are a sports reporter," said Maya, which made Grace beam.

"What about you?" Dad asked Maya. "Have you ever thought about the future?"

"I only want to help make the world a better place

somehow," she said. She didn't think it was a good idea to mention that Dr. Jenkins was her new hero. She thought of Bijou. "Maybe travel. Make friends all over the world."

"Well," said Dad. "You might be pleasantly surprised tomorrow."

* * *

Maya felt like she was heading toward the Death Star as they walked across the vast parking lot to Alceria's main entrance. She had been to the Alceria campus, but not for a long time. The lobby was vast, with skylights three stories high casting rays of light on ornamental fountains. As a little kid, she had climbed up on the ledges of the fountains and dangled her fingertips in the frothy water. She still wanted to.

"So this is the girl!" a man said in the lobby. Dad nodded but didn't reply. They took the elevator to the fifth floor and walked up the hall to Dad's office. He shared the space with a younger man named Jake, who was already at his desk and clattering away on the keys. His computer tower was lined up with Lego Minifigures: Batman, Spider-Man, Indiana Jones.

"Hey, kids," Jake said, barely looking at them. "I hear you're stars of Web and screen. Got any movie deals yet?"

"Wait until my album drops," said Maya, playing along.

"I'm launching a fragrance," Grace added.

"Oh, I launched a fragrance myself," said Jake, fanning the air with his hand.

"Gross!" Grace said with a laugh. Dad shot him a look.

"Sorry," said Jake. "Anyway, it's great to see you both. Good luck today." He turned back to his computer.

"Why do we need luck?" Grace whispered to Maya.

* * *

The morning passed slowly. They walked down hallway after hallway, rode up and down elevators, and were introduced to a bunch of people with names Maya wouldn't remember and job titles she didn't understand. Most of the people they passed in the halls were men, but most of the people Dad introduced them to were women. He was probably trying to show them that Alceria was a good place for women to work.

Even besides the bee killing, there was something about the place that made Maya nervous. Everybody seemed overdressed for summer and overeager to prove themselves. Men were quick to make jokes, and women too quick to smile and compliment her and Grace. More than once, somebody referred to her as "the girl."

They know about the TV show, she thought. They all know. When Dad had said he'd been watching it with his work group and boss, she'd assumed those were the only people at Alceria who had seen the show. Had she been the subject of staff meetings and office memos? "Tomorrow morning, the girl who tried to destroy this company will be visiting. Please offer fake smiles and be nice to her."

A couple of people asked her if she was excited about the presentation. "Sure," she said, even though she had no idea what the presentation was about. Why would she be excited about some business thing? It was probably going to be some guy bragging about how Alceria had sold more stuff this year than last year and expected to sell even more stuff next year.

They had lunch in the cafeteria, and Dad got them each an oversize cookie when they were done. It made Maya feel like a spoiled little kid, walking toward his office with the giant cookie. Instead of taking the elevator, they walked through the atrium and joined a river of people heading down another long hallway toward a row of doors. They strolled through to an auditorium with theater-style seating that ramped downward to the stage.

The presentation, Maya realized. The whole company seemed to be invited.

They sat in the front of the auditorium, staring at a gigantic plasma screen that was currently showing the Alceria logo.

"Wow," said Grace. "Wish the new Avengers movie was showing on that thing."

When a gray-haired man came to the podium to address the audience, Maya felt like he was looking right at her. Of course he wasn't, she told herself. He was looking out to the room. But it sure seemed like he was looking at her.

"You probably know who I am," he said, and the audience laughed, then clapped.

"He's the CEO," Dad whispered.

"Thank you all for taking time out of your day to be here," he said, but Maya had a feeling nobody had a choice. "As you know, I'm totally committed to three things. Well, four. The first is this company, and the important work we do, and all of you. The second is my family. The third, as many of you know, is golf— but that is an unrequited love." The audience laughed a lot harder than the joke deserved. "The fourth," he said, "is the environment. I share this passion with my entire family. We spend so much time traveling to beautiful, unspoiled parts of the world, many of them right here in Minnesota."

And now the screen came to life. There was a slide show of Minnesota scenery: prairie grass and wildflowers, loons gliding down to splash in ponds, the sun setting behind some trees, a fox trotting in the snow (Maya's heart felt a twinge), a flock of herons taking to the sky. Stirring music played.

"And that," said the CEO, "is why I'm thrilled to tell you about Alceria's newest venture, which is the restoration and preservation of one thousand acres of native prairie, right here in our own backyard."

A map came up, showing where an L shape of green space would fit snugly into a western corner of Minneapolis, stretching almost to Maya's own neighborhood. The caption read, *Alceria Prairie Garden.*

"This is only the beginning," said the CEO. "Alceria is committed to prairieland restoration and preservation around the state, and will eventually restore another ten thousand acres of prairie in central Minnesota."

A new map popped up, showing a sprawl of green

between Minneapolis and Saint Cloud. The audience cheered. *Alceria Nature Preserve* read the caption.

"Wow," said Grace. "Ten thousand acres."

Versus how many millions of acres of tainted crops? Maya wondered.

"And so," said the CEO, "as we continue to strive to feed the world, we want to send a clear message that Alceria cares about our planet and everyone who lives here." The screen showed buffalo thundering across a plain and then switched to a close-up of a bee collecting pollen from a wildflower. "Whatever their size!"

* * *

"Pretty great, huh?" asked their dad as they walked toward the elevators. "Do you see why I thought today was the perfect one for a visit?"

"It's awesome," said Grace. "It's like your garden, only a million times bigger."

"Sure," said Maya. "It's great." It was, she told herself, so why wasn't she excited?

"It's been in the works for ages," Dad said. "I knew about it, but we weren't allowed to talk about it until everything was official—all the land purchased, the agreements signed, you know. It's quite a big operation. Probably cost the company a million dollars."

They got on the elevator, which was now full of people heading back to their offices from the presentation.

"Are you excited about the nature preserve?" somebody asked Maya.

"Sure," she said. "It's going to be lovely." Everyone on the elevator smiled and nodded.

When they reached Dad's floor, he stopped them from getting off.

"One more stop," he said. "Then we can take off. I already cleared it with my supervisor."

The elevator gradually emptied until they were the only ones left. They got off on the twelfth floor—high enough to see most of the city when they glanced out the windows across from the elevators. There was another fountain here and a couple of potted trees. Maya glanced in a fountain and saw fat koi swimming around. They continued through a set of glass doors. A woman stood to greet them.

"He'll be here shortly," she said. "You can sit down right here."

There was only one person they could be meeting on the top floor in this massive suite.

Sure enough, the gray-haired man from the presentation came striding in.

"Michael," he said to Maya's dad. He shook her dad's hand, grabbing his elbow with his other hand to make it especially chummy. He turned his attention to her and Grace. "And these are your beautiful daughters. Excellent. I'm so pleased to meet both of you. Right this way—my office is too dreary, so let's go to the conference room. Coffee and cookies?" He suggested the last to the receptionist, who nodded.

Maya hadn't been able to finish her first cookie and hoped she wouldn't have to eat another one to be polite.

They sat in stuffed leather chairs, Grace swiveling back and forth.

"Nice," she said.

"Have you ever been up here before?" Maya asked her father.

"Of course," he said. "Many times."

The CEO (Maya still didn't know his name) took his own chair, put his elbows on the table, and leaned in.

"So," he said. "What do you think of our prairie garden?"

"Really amazing," said Grace.

"Wonderful," said Maya. "Thanks for doing it." Was that all he wanted? To soak up their gratitude? Or was he expecting her to apologize?

"Has your father talked to you about the—" He saw Dad shaking his head. "Ah, well. Then let me tell you. You know that Alceria has suffered a few smears lately. Gossip travels at ten times the speed of information, so it's hard to keep up. We hope that this plan sends a clear message of where Alceria stands on environmental issues."

"It does," said Grace. Maya, aware that all eyes were on her, forced herself to nod.

"We also hope that by doing this, we can win over some of our most vocal critics," he said. "We don't expect Dr. Jenkins to do a promotional spot for us, but perhaps children are a bit more open-minded…"

"You want us to do a commercial?" Maya interrupted.

"It's not a commercial exactly," he said. "Well, sure. Yes. It's a commercial. An excited child running across a knoll of native grass, like that kid on the TV show…not that I'm expecting you to wear a pioneer dress or anything…"

"What?"

"Maybe that show was before your time."

"I know what you're talking about," said Grace. "*Little House on the Prairie.*"

"You want us to dress like pioneer children?" Maya asked.

"None of that has been decided," said the CEO, waving his palm. "The ad agency will come up with something. But because I care so much, you know, about the environment. About your little pollinators." He looked right at Maya. "I wanted to extend the invitation myself."

A man came in with a cart and put out a pot of coffee and a tray of cookies. An entire tray for four people. How many cookies did he think she and Grace would eat? Her father poured half a paper cup of coffee and stirred in creamer.

"You don't have to answer immediately," said the CEO. "I'll give you your privacy so you can discuss this as a family." He stood up. "I have another meeting anyway. A little confab with the bean counters. I'll check back in a little while, or you can leave a message for me with Darla."

"Sure," said Dad.

"Michael, it was great to see you again."

"You too," said Dad.

The head honcho of Alceria left the room.

"Of course I would never make you do something

like this," said Dad, "but I don't think I have to tell you how much it would mean to me, or, uh, how much it would mean for my future at Alceria."

"I'm in," said Grace. "I never hated Alceria in the first place."

They both turned to face Maya, who stalled by taking a cookie from the tray.

CHAPTER 35

"You don't have to say anything you don't believe," Dad said as he pulled out of the parking lot, looking up in the rearview mirror so he could see her. "For example, you can say that bees are important to our future, and maybe the videographer has footage of you twirling around in the garden or whatever…"

"Nobody said anything about twirling," said Grace in the passenger seat.

"You don't have to twirl," said Dad. He looked back to Maya. "You can use this to get your message out. That's what I'm saying. If you think about it, Alceria isn't only giving you a garden—"

"They aren't *giving me* the garden," said Maya.

"You know what I mean. They're doing the garden plus the nature preserve, plus you get a free PSA to talk about bees."

"Dad, I said I would do it," she said. "You don't have to persuade me."

"I want you to feel good about it too," said Dad.

"I don't feel good about it," she said. "But I said I'll do it, and I'll smile and be nice. I'll even twirl, if that's what they want. OK?"

"Yes. OK. Thank you."

She thought about what kids at school would say after seeing the commercial and felt sick to her stomach.

"There's a Barnes and Noble over by the mall," said Dad. "Do you want to drop by?"

"Nah." She didn't want Dad to buy her anything. It made her feel like even more of a traitor. What was she supposed to do? If she said no, Dad would be mad at her, and he'd be in trouble at work. Meanwhile, Alceria would go right on making neonicotinoids and killing bees. They would make the commercial with the children of a more loyal employee and pretend they cared about the environment.

"So what did you think of the visit otherwise?" Dad asked. "Lots of great people, huh?"

"Sure." Maya had to give her dad that much. People were nice to her all day.

"Good people, doing good work. That's all I wanted you to see," said Dad.

* * *

The next day it rained heavily, with lightning flashing against a gloomy sky. Maya was disappointed she couldn't go on a bike ride. Grace didn't have to work, so she settled on the couch with a copy of *Seabiscuit*.

"I didn't know you cared about horse racing," said Maya.

"I don't, but it's a bestselling sports book by a woman," said Grace. "Besides, it's good even if you don't care about horse racing."

Since the computer was free, Maya logged on to her private email.

She saw Bijou's name in the contacts list, and the green light that showed she was online. She clicked on it, then selected the video chat icon. Moments later a window opened. There was the skinny girl from the photo, only older. Her face was serious, her eyes intense. Behind her was a tiny cluttered room. Maya had never really been worried that Bijou wasn't who she said she was, but it was amazing to actually see her.

"Hi!" said Maya. "I wanted to say I understand—"

Bijou shook her head and frowned, then said something Maya couldn't hear.

Maya fumbled with the settings but couldn't get the audio to play.

The girls gestured helplessly at each other until Maya started laughing at her own improvised sign language. At last a smile cracked across Bijou's serious expression. She started fluttering her fingers around, making them into crazed birds while Maya laughed.

Even though they couldn't talk, it was hard to hang up.

* * *

"I've got news," Dad announced at dinner. "Mr. Patterson wanted to thank you for agreeing to do his commercial. He knows you girls are big baseball fans, so he's letting you have the Alceria suite at Target Field for a game. I've never seen it, but last year the sales department went, and Scott told me it was stunning. He said there's a gorgeous view of the field and the food is amazing. And you can invite up to thirty people."

"I don't know thirty people," said Maya.

"I do," said Grace, her eyes brightening. "I could have a Thinking Girl meet-up."

"You want to meet those blog people in real life?" Mom asked.

"What do you mean, those blog people? They're regular people like me."

"I'm sure most of them are," Mom said after a moment. "I mean, I know you have good judgment."

"This will be awesome," said Grace.

Maya didn't like being indebted to Mr. Patterson, but she couldn't refuse his offer and take it away from her sister.

"That sounds like fun," she said. "But I'd rather see the rabbits."

"What rabbits?" Dad asked.

"Did you even read the blog that caused all the fuss?" Grace asked.

"Oh right. Of course I did," he said. He plunged his fork into his spaghetti and gave it a twirl. "OK, so we'll go to Cedar Rapids too."

"Really? All of us?" Maya didn't believe it.

"Sure. We'll look at a calendar," said Dad. "Find a time that works for everybody..."

"No," said Maya. "Next week."

"Um, sure," he said. "I mean, I can look at my schedule and..."

"Wednesday," said Maya.

"Why Wednesday?"

"Because it's a day game," said Maya. "We can drive home right after the game without being up until 2:00 a.m."

"I can help drive," Grace offered.

"Well, of course I need to coordinate with..." Dad started, before he saw Maya's eyes and quit mid-sentence.

"I'll make it work," he said. "And now, um, now for the other news. They want to make the commercial tomorrow."

CHAPTER 36

The ad agency was in a row of buildings that included a drugstore, a coffee shop, and an upscale grocery. It looked harmless enough, but Maya felt like she was in a horror movie, approaching a tall, gloomy castle on top of a craggy hill.

"Are you sure you want to do this?" Dad asked after pulling into the guest parking spot in front of the agency.

"I don't mind," Grace answered quickly.

"I'll do it," said Maya. "I don't want to do it, but I'll do it."

"That's how I feel most days," Dad admitted.

The ad agency was weird and arty. There was a pool table in the middle of the lobby for no reason. The balls on the table looked arranged, not like a game had been abandoned. Elaborate mobiles had been strung from the ceiling.

Maya looked down and realized she was wearing the same skirt and sweater she'd worn on TV. Would anyone notice? Did it matter?

"Hello, hello!" A youngish man with floppy hair came out to greet them. He was wearing an expensive-looking shirt and ratty jeans that probably cost more than the shirt. "I'm Noel. Let me show you to the green room."

Another green room, thought Maya. I wonder if it's green.

It wasn't. It was a muted brown with a slash of magenta. Maya was glad the refrigerator had bottled water instead of something conceptual, like fish bowls full of Windex. She opened one, swigged it, and hoped she would get through this thing without having to pee. Too late, she remembered that plastic water bottles were awful for the environment.

Dad stood out of the way, studying a row of framed ads the agency must have created: a cartoonish copy of that famous painting *The Scream*, ants smothering an apple core, a pseudo-superhero standing atop a parking ramp with cape billowing in the air. Maya couldn't see what the ads were *for*. Dad could, but looked no less perplexed.

A woman came in holding a clipboard.

"I'm Staci," she said. "Super excited to meet you." She was all lipstick and teeth. Maya did have to pee. Why did she agree to this? Because of Dad, she reminded herself. He turned from the wall of ad art.

"Hello," he said. "I'm the girls' father."

"We made some last-minute decisions, and we won't need the older girl," said Staci. "We love your look," she told Grace. "But we think it'll be stronger with one actor."

Grace started to say something, but shook her head and settled down on one of the Adirondack chairs. "I love your look too," she said finally.

"Thank you!" said Staci. She reached out and put her hand on Maya's shoulder. Maya couldn't help but notice the swirls of color on Staci's fingernails and wondered how long that took. Maybe they weren't painted though, she thought. Maybe they were decals, like some of the girls at school wore. She realized Staci had been speaking. She hadn't heard a word.

"Sorry?"

"We'll talk through the copy, then do the voice-over," she said. "Then we'll do two really short video takes. One for the beginning of the spot and one for the end. It's a thirty-second spot so the whole thing should take…" She thought it over. "Three hours?"

"Three hours for thirty seconds?" Dad asked in surprise.

"If we're lucky," said Staci. "Here's the final copy." She handed Maya three loose pages of double-spaced type. Staci was wearing a scent that reminded Maya simultaneously of her wildflower garden and the last time Mom cleaned the floors. It made her eyes sting. She tried to read the copy, but the words swam on the page. She took a sip of water and looked again.

> The environment isn't only the rain forests and oceans. It's also right here in Minnesota. That's why Alceria is making an investment in the future of our beautiful state. The Alceria prairie restoration project will restore almost five hundred acres...

She stopped. Five hundred? Mr. Patterson had said a thousand in the presentation.

> ...almost five hundred acres of natural prairieland in the heart of Minneapolis, and thousands more in the surrounding area.

Thousands was vague. Had they cut back on that promise too?

As a preserver of plant and animal life, Alceria guarantees that the natural splendor of the prairies will be around for generations to wonder at and enjoy. Because Alceria cares.

"I can't say this," she said. Dad looked at her. She thought he might interrupt, but he didn't.

"That copy is final," said Staci. "It's been approved by the client, so..."

"I'll say all of it except the last three words," said Maya. "I can't say that part."

"Why not?"

"Because I don't think it's true." She looked at Dad instead of Staci. He seemed to wince.

"Oh, honey," said Staci. "We're not a truth agency. We're an advertising agency."

"Can I see the copy?" Dad asked.

Maya handed him the pages, and he flipped through them quickly. Grace tried to read over his shoulder.

"I'll say it," she volunteered. "Maya can still be the one on camera. I can even talk like her." She raised her voice a little and sounded more like Minnie Mouse.

"I don't talk like that!" said Maya.

"I don't talk like that," Grace mimicked, still sounding like Minnie Mouse.

"Grace," Dad cautioned.

"Never mind," said Maya. Her lower lip trembled. "I'll do it. I'll do all of it."

She glanced up and saw her father looking at her, his eyes filled with sadness. His Adam's apple bobbed.

"Hold on," he said. He got his smartphone out and made a call.

"Hi Darla, it's Michael Sutton," he said. "Is Mr. Patterson available? Yes, it is. All right." He held up two fingers. "Hi. You too. Yes, we're here now. Absolutely. The thing is, we're not going to do it. No, I mean ever. Yes, I'm serious. No, we can't talk about it. Because they don't want to do it. Absolutely. Yep. Three o'clock. I'll be there. You too. Bye."

Staci stared at him, her mouth hanging open.

He tapped the phone to hang up. "I have to drop you girls off, then go back to the office to get fired. But we do have time for lunch."

CHAPTER 37

Dad didn't get fired after all. Mr. Patterson had only wanted to meet to say he was sorry for putting pressure on him and his daughters, to say that Alceria really wasn't that kind of a company, and he wanted to know if Dad was otherwise happy. But somehow, by the end of the meeting, Dad had resigned.

"He sort of talked me into it while acting like he was begging me not to," Dad explained at dinner. He'd picked up food at their favorite takeout place, a Thai restaurant a mile away.

"I don't understand," said Grace.

"I do," said Mom.

"I don't want to work there anymore," said Dad. He glanced at Maya—not with the doting look of a dad, she thought, but with respect. "Asking my daughter to compromise her integrity was the last straw." He'd been ignoring his food and finally speared a ring of calamari.

"So what happens now?" asked Grace.

"They say I can serve out my notice at home," said Dad. "But they locked me out of all the computers and didn't give me anything to do, so I guess I'll spend the time updating my résumé and signing up for LinkedIn."

"Watch out," said Grace. "That might be a gateway to Facebook."

"Ha. I sure hope not."

Maya knew she should be worried, but it was hard when she was eating her favorite restaurant meal—the cranberry curry from My Thai—on a day her father had stood up for her.

"Plus we have a baseball game," she reminded him.

"Right," said Dad. "I can't wait."

* * *

Maya listened to the Kernels night game with headphones. Rafael was pulled in the seventh inning, after getting zero hits in four at bats. Now the game was tied in the thirteenth inning. For some reason, Maya wanted to see it through before she went to bed.

A new window popped up.

Bijou has invited you to chat.

Maya: Hi. You're up late.

Bijou: I'm on the office computer listening to the game. Rafael is still slumping. :-(

Maya: I know. I hope he turns it around soon.

Bijou: He's always been like that. Up and down.

Maya: Hey! I'll see him again in person in a few days. Our family is going to a Kernels game. They're playing the Rattlers so I'll see Juan too.

Bijou: Really?

Maya: Yep. He's not pitching though. I don't think.

Because she was thinking about Juan, Maya opened the photo and looked at it yet again. She was pretty sure that the boy next to Rafael was Juan, and that the bigger boy was his older brother. But she didn't have any proof and wanted to know if she was right. Would Bijou get mad at her if she asked? She didn't want to ruin their friendship.

But that was part of why she wanted to ask. She didn't want her friend lying to her.

Maya: Bijou, can I be honest?

Bijou: Claro. That means, of course.

Maya: I don't think that pitcher for the Rattlers is Juan. I think he is Juan's brother.

For a long time she saw: "Bijou is typing." If it was taking her so long to answer, Maya thought, it must be true. At last the message appeared.

Bijou: You're correct. He is Hugo Santos Garcia. Juan's older brother.

Maya felt a flood of relief that Bijou trusted her, along with icy fear—real fear—that she now knew a secret.

Maya: Thanks for telling me, B.

Bijou: Have you told anyone? It would ruin many lives, including mine, if you did. My father might get fired. We would get thrown out on the street.

Maya: No, I haven't told a soul.

Bijou: Promise you won't! Especially your sister. She could put in her blog.

Maya started typing that she wouldn't tell anybody, but stopped. Could she promise that? What if she blurted it out? What did it mean to keep a secret like this? She took a deep breath. She wished she could go back in time and never ask, to have her suspicions but no proof.

Bijou: Are you still there?

Maya: I need to think. I'll write soon, OK? & I won't do anything until I talk to you again.

She closed the window, but an email appeared before she could sign out.

Maya,

Sorry I was so bossy. I am scared of what might happen. But I am your friend no matter what you do. I hope you know that.

Bijou

CHAPTER 38

Rafael, Five Years Ago

One day, Carlos drove Rafael to the suburb of Ramon Santana where the Brewers had their facilities. Rafael had a good tryout. It was his sixth in as many days.

"He's a mature player," said the Brewers scout. "Are you sure he's only fourteen?"

"Thirteen for another month," said Carlos. "I've seen his papers. He's on the level."

"How long have you known him?"

"Since he was eleven."

They had this conversation as if Rafael wasn't standing right there.

"He doesn't look older than fourteen," the scout agreed. "I think with his intelligence and ability, he'll be a good prospect. Maybe not a million-dollar prospect but a good prospect. Do you want to retain agency?"

Rafael knew that meant Carlos might sell his share of Rafael's future outright.

"It depends on what he wants," Carlos said. "I only want to be sure of his future. After three years, he's like a *sobrino*." Rafael wondered if that was true. Did Carlos think of him as a nephew, or was it typical buscone talk, meant to drive a harder bargain?

The two men lowered their voices, and Rafael wandered off to see other boys taking at bats for the scouts. The academy in Ramon Santana was the nicest he'd seen yet. The grass was lusher, the equipment newer. He hoped Carlos would work out a deal.

"Rafael! *Vamos*!" Carlos called.

He hurried over.

"What happened?"

"They like you a lot," said Carlos, walking across the gravel parking lot toward the truck.

Once they were on the way home, he said more.

"This might be the best offer you get, but we still have the trip to Boca Chica. Do you want to accept now or see the other academies?"

Rafael fought the urge to accept now. What if the men changed their mind? What if a bunch of new boys showed up and took all the open spots?

"I should talk to Papa first," he said.

"Smart boy," said Carlos. "By the way, that man said they accepted your friend Juan."

"Really?"

"They're really impressed," said Carlos. "Guess I was wrong about him."

* * *

Rafael ran to Juan's house as soon as they got back to the city. Juan was out on the curb.

"Juan, we might be teammates!" Rafael said excitedly. He blurted out everything that had happened in Ramon Santana.

Juan's face was serious.

"What's wrong?" Rafael wondered if the academy had changed their mind about Juan, or if Carlos had misunderstood.

"Rafi, I have a big secret. You'll find out anyway so I'll tell you. But you can't tell anyone."

"What?"

"They didn't accept *me*," said Juan. "They accepted Hugo."

"But Hugo's sixteen. He should be trying out to get signed right now, not applying for the academy."

"He used my birth certificate." Juan grinned,

though the news was nothing to smile about. "Now he is Juan Santos Garcia."

"Oh." Rafael knew such things happened. "But they've already seen him," he recalled. "He tried out two years ago." Maybe nobody would remember him, but if even one person did, he would be finished. He would be banned for a year and come back a year older with a black mark against him.

"Hugo *didn't* try out," Juan explained. "*Damian* tried out, using Hugo's name." He shrugged. "I think they were disappointed. He was not as good as they heard. But now they hear, wait until you see his little brother." He mimed a pitch. "*Juan* will be a superstar."

"You planned it that far back?"

"Hugo's agent did. It was his idea. He's sharp, that man. He made me become a pitcher so I could show up...I mean, Hugo could show up. Ah, you know what I mean!"

Rafael felt the ground crumbling beneath his feet. He didn't care if Hugo cheated a little. Hugo was a great player, and it wasn't fair he was hurt two years ago. But if Damian was Hugo, and Hugo was Juan...

"Who are you going to be? How are you going to try out?"

"I'm not going to be anybody." Juan held out his

hands in mock surrender. "I don't even need to because Hugo will be…" He rubbed his fingers together, miming someone with a lot of cash.

"That's not fair," said Rafael. "You deserve a shot too."

"Rafael!" Juan put his hand on Rafael's shoulder. "Rafi, I don't have Hugo's hands or your fever. Everybody knows that but you. Papa, Hugo, me, Romero, Cádiz, even Carlos. I was only in the academy for the cover story. My birth certificate has more value right now than all of the rest of me."

"But we were supposed to do this together." Rafael looked down the street. He could see the glaring red of the sun blurred by smog. What a day. He was going to an academy, and from there, he'd probably get a deal. He wasn't just a kid fantasizing anymore. It was all laid out in front of him. But he'd always imagined Juan would be there too. This was like getting a toy he'd dreamed about and then finding out it was damaged. Not enough so it didn't work, but a little chip or crack that spoiled the magic. "It won't be the same," he said.

"It's all good," said Juan. If he was upset deep down inside, he didn't show it. "You and Hugo both made it. Hermano, this is the best day of my life."

"Sure," said Rafael. He tried to be as happy as Juan.

His friend had even called him a brother. That would have put him on the moon a few years ago.

Now it reminded him that he had a real brother too.

He stood up. "I better go tell my family about the academy. See you tomorrow?"

"No, I have to disappear for a while," said Juan. "Going to stay with family in Yamasá. If the team sends people to check on Hugo's story, they can't find another Juan hanging around."

"Then I'll see you when you reappear," said Rafael.

"Remember me when you're rich and famous?"

"I will," said Rafael. "I might even come back to the barrio and give you a cap."

Both boys laughed hard.

"I can't wait," said Juan.

The boys clapped hands, and Rafael set off for home. After a few seconds, he started to run.

* * *

"I got into an academy!" he shouted the moment he entered the house.

"I know," said Papa. He was sitting in the armchair instead of working. He had quit early today for some reason. Rafael slowly walked over, looking around.

"Where are Mama and Iván?"

"Mama went to the colmado, and Iván's off in the street somewhere."

Rafael felt his happiness wilt. At Juan's house, the whole family waited by the phone, talking excitedly. Here, Papa hardly seemed to care, and nobody else was even home.

"Papa, this is a big deal." Why did Rafael have to explain that? He must be the only boy in the Dominican Republic who did.

"I know," his father said evenly. "Carlos said this Brewers academy is nice."

"It is. But I'll try out at a couple more. We might get other offers."

His father peered at him.

"He said your friend Juan is at the same academy. I thought you'd want to go with your best friend."

Rafael didn't answer. He suddenly realized he couldn't go to the Brewers academy. He couldn't see Hugo every day and call him Juan. That would be too hard.

"What's the problem?" Papa asked.

"Papa, Juan..." Rafael's voice fell to a whisper. His father leaned in to listen. Rafael wasn't supposed to tell anyone, but his father would keep the secret. "Juan didn't really get in," he burst out. He told his father about how Hugo had cheated his way in.

"I see," Papa said. He put a hand on Rafael's shoulder and drew him closer. He wrapped his arms around him the way he did when Rafael was little. "I'm sorry your friend can't go with you." Usually he would go into a lecture, but this time he did not. Rafael could not stop his tears. Papa let him cry on his shoulder. After a few minutes, he nudged Rafael away. "But this is supposed to be a celebration," he said. "Don't let Mama see you like this. She'll be back soon with the food and balloons."

"Really? You're having a party for me?"

"Yes. And Iván is gathering your friends from the neighborhood. Sorry to spoil the surprise, but it's better than everyone walking in and finding my victorious boy bawling and covered with snot."

Rafael's sob turned to a laugh. He dried his eyes on the hem of his shirt. "Papa, I thought you guys didn't care."

"Of course we do," said Papa. "We worry, is all."

"That I won't make it?" Rafael asked.

"That we'll lose you," his father said softly. "Now be festive."

The door burst open, and soon the house filled up with people.

CHAPTER 39

Maya

Maya was dying to talk to somebody, but she couldn't tell Grace about the scandal. Bijou had asked her specifically not to. Maya didn't think Grace would tell anyone, but who knew? Maybe she would see it as a chance to get a byline in a major magazine or a blog post with thousands of hits. One she'd written herself this time.

She found Dad at the kitchen table the next morning, browsing through job listings. He tried to shut the laptop before Maya saw what he was doing, but she noticed the logo in the upper left.

"You're looking for a job at NASA?"

"They must need data crunchers," he said almost apologetically. "But I don't see anything I'm qualified for, and besides, I don't want to move. What's up?"

She sat down across the table from him.

"Dad, what if I knew a big secret? Like, I found out that somebody stole some money from a company that he—or she—worked for. Not that exactly, but something like that."

"Your sister didn't dip into the till at the DQ, did she?"

"No! Grace would never do that, Dad! How can you even think it?"

"Well, you're the one who put the idea in my head," he said. He glanced into his coffee cup and saw it was empty. "But you're right. Grace would never do that." He stood up and poured a bit more coffee from the pot, then sat down again. Maya traced the whorled pattern on the tablecloth with her finger. It was like solving an infinite maze.

"Dad, this is for a lot of money. Millions of dollars."

Dad blinked, and it took him a moment to make words again. "Honey, did you witness something? You're not in any danger, are you?"

"No. I figured it out on my own and confirmed it with somebody who knows."

"But you're not in any danger?"

"No, the culpr…the person who did it doesn't even know I exist."

"You have a much more interesting life than I thought," he said. He sipped his coffee. "I'd say if you know about a crime and don't tell anyone, you're kind of an accessory."

"Really?" That was not what she wanted to hear. "What if the culprit is really a nice person, and the company he stole from is awful?" She wished she knew a nicer word for *culprit*.

Dad gave her a narrow look. "Honey, do you think I stole money from Alceria?"

"No," she said. "Of course not." She was doing a terrible job of explaining. She didn't know if Hugo was such a nice guy, anyway, and she certainly didn't think that the Brewers were awful. Maybe closed-minded about signing older players, but that didn't make them evil. She stood up and fixed herself a raisin bagel with cream cheese and honey. It had been a favorite snack for Claire, and now she was hooked. Dad left his laptop closed.

"What have you gotten yourself mixed up in, Maya?" he asked when she sat down again.

"It's a baseball thing." She explained between bites of gooey bagel. She didn't say any names, positions, or teams.

"And you know this because…"

"I did research," she said. "And I had it confirmed by a friend in the DR who knows the player."

"You have a friend in the DR?"

Maya nodded. "We met online." Dad nearly jumped out of his chair.

"You're talking to strange men in other countries?"

"It's not a man. It's a girl," Maya said. "She's Grace's age."

"Well, sure. That's what *he* says."

Maya couldn't help but laugh. "We video chatted. She is who she says she is."

"You video chatted," he mouthed, then shook his head. "Is it your favorite player? The guy you blogged about."

"No," she said. "I swear it's not him. It's somebody else."

"Hmm." Dad mulled it over. "I don't really see this as embezzlement. More like stowing away on a ship. Using somebody else's ticket, you know? Hardly a capital crime."

"But this ticket came with a three-million-dollar bonus, Dad."

"Oh? Wow." He mulled it over some more. "I still

don't see it as the crime of the century, but it's a lot of money to take under false pretenses."

"I don't know what to do. Should I tell someone or not? Either way I feel terrible."

"Grown-ups make choices like that every day," he said. "I wish they all put as much thought into it as you're doing now."

"I'm tired of thinking about it," she admitted.

"Listen, if you do tell, we're here for you, OK? We can run interference if the phone keeps ringing or whatever."

"Thanks, Dad."

"And if you choose not to tell, I understand."

"Thanks." She sniffed. "You quit your job so I wouldn't have to 'compromise my integrity,' and now I have this great big lie I'm a part of."

"Is that the only reason you *would* tell?"

Maya thought about it and nodded. "Yeah. Mostly."

"Then don't," he said. "You have the most integrity of anyone I know."

CHAPTER 40

Maya was swept up in the excitement of baseball once they got to the ballpark: the smell of fried food wafting from the concourse and the sight of the diamond from the bleachers. The Rattlers were now out for batting practice, so she couldn't see Rafael, but it was a relief to see his name posted on the scoreboard for the home team lineup. All the way to Cedar Rapids, she'd worried that they'd arrive at the ballpark and find out he'd been cut that morning.

"There's Monica." Grace waved so the reporter could find them. The frizzy-haired woman saw them, smiled, and started up the steps.

"Did she know we would be here?" Maya asked.

"We traded emails," Grace explained in a whisper.

"Hi!" Monica said when she reached their seats. "You have amazing kids," she said to Mom and Dad.

"We know it," said Mom. Dad nodded.

"So, do you want to come to the press box?" she asked Maya. "It'll be easier to talk."

"Huh?" said Maya.

"Just go," said Grace.

"Go," said Mom. "Go."

Maya and Grace followed Monica to a covered area at the top of the bleachers directly behind home plate. There was a row of chairs behind a long desk facing the field. The view was excellent.

A young guy looked up from his laptop. "Those must be the girls."

"These are the girls," Monica confirmed. "Grace and Maya, this is Mike. And that's—"

Maya realized who else was in the press box and didn't need to be told who it was. Rafael Rosales was at the far end of the room, filling a cone-shaped cup from a water cooler. He had already been out on the field and was damp with perspiration. She could smell his sweat and see it glistening on his lip.

"Hello," he said in practiced English. "Very pleased to meet you."

"*Mucho gusto!*" said Grace with zeal.

Rafael downed the water, crumpled the cup in his

hand, and dropped it in the wastebasket.

"Mike, time to show us what you can do," said Monica.

"Spanish minor in college," he explained. He spoke to Rafael, and Rafael answered.

"He says he has to be back in the clubhouse in ten minutes," said Mike.

"Then let's do the picture first." Monica posed the three of them, Rafael's sweaty arms tossed around their shoulders. He's muscular, thought Maya. Of course he was. He was a professional athlete who could knock five-ounce rubber balls over fences four hundred feet away. After the photo was done, she wasn't sure if she'd smiled.

"Rafael, did you read the story Maya wrote about your first game here?" Monica asked. Mike repeated the question in Spanish, and Rafael answered.

"He says a friend translated for him," Mike translated, "and he liked it very much."

Maya swallowed hard. Somehow, even having reached a friend of Rafael's, she hadn't thought of her words reaching Rafael himself.

Rafael talked some more. "He says he is sorry about your garden," Mike translated. "He wants to know if you'll plant it again next year."

"I hadn't thought about it," Maya admitted. But she could start over, couldn't she? Some of the flowers and forbs might come back on their own, and the chemicals would have worn off by then.

Rafael spoke to Mike.

"He says you better grow it, so he can see it when he gets called up to Minneapolis."

"That means he has to make it all the way up to the Twins," said Maya.

Mike had a short exchange with Rafael.

"He says it's a deal."

"Deal," Maya agreed.

Rafael spoke some more. "He has to go," said Mike. "He says he's sorry he doesn't have more time."

"Claro," said Maya. Rafael smiled at her one word of Spanish. He clasped her hand briefly, then Grace's, and was out the door.

"He seems like a decent guy," said Mike. "I hope things turn out for him."

"Me too," Monica agreed.

"Thank you so much for setting that up," Maya told Monica. "That was amazing."

"Happy to do it," said Monica.

But Maya started to have regrets the moment she

and Grace left the press box. She felt like she'd blown the opportunity to really *talk* to Rafael. There were a million things she could have asked: What was his childhood like? What did his parents do? Did he ever get homesick? Did he have brothers or sisters? Instead, he'd asked about her garden, and she'd never gotten the chance. And now she had to plant it again, on the one-in-a-million chance that he made it to the major leagues and kept his promise.

But he'd asked her about her garden, and that was sweet. He'd treated her like a friend, not like a fan.

"Hey, there's no crying in baseball," Grace teased.

"Shut up. I'm not crying." But she was tearing up, and she knew it.

Only after they sat down did Maya remember that she had not written about the garden in her blog entry. Rafael could only know about that from Bijou. Bijou must be the friend that had translated the story for him. Was it in a friendly email? An urgent phone call? Did Rafael know what she knew? Maya had so much to think about that it was the third or fourth inning before she noticed the action on the field. Grace was suddenly standing up and hooting and cheering. Everybody was. The scoreboard was showing a graphic of fireworks exploding, and flashed the word WOW! Maya stood up and cheered too, but it wasn't until she sat down that she realized what had happened. Rafael had hit a home run.

"I guess the slump is over," said Grace.

"It's just one hit," said Maya. "We'll have to wait and see."

"Ha." Grace gave her a surprised look. "I think you've officially graduated from fledgling fan to seasoned cynic."

Maya shrugged. She knew better than to get her hopes too high.

She looked down to the visitors' bull pen and saw Juan-not-Juan getting his work in, as the Twins broadcaster would call it. He wasn't pitching today but had to keep his arm loose for the next time he did.

"I'll be right back. Don't let Rafael hit any more home runs until I return."

"I'll see what I can do," Grace said with a laugh.

Maya strolled around the concourse, stopping for a metallic-tasting drink of water from a fountain and to get her nerve up. The visiting team's bull pen was in front of some bleachers that seemed to have been added to the stadium as an afterthought. Right now, they were full of little kids in bright-yellow T-shirts. They must have been part of a day camp or youth group. A row of steps ran down the middle, and at the bottom, you could practically reach out and snatch the caps off the visiting team. She felt nervous going down, sure somebody would stop her, but aside from kids darting back and forth across the steps in front of her, she reached the fence with no problem.

What would she say? Would he even know English?

With every throw, she could hear the snap of the ball as it hit the catcher's glove. The pitcher stopped, did some stretching exercises, saw her, and nodded.

"Hola!" she said. She also knew *Adiós*, so she had the front and back end of the conversation covered. Everything in between was a problem.

"Do you want an autograph?" he asked in accented English.

"Sure," she said. But she didn't have a pen or anything to sign. She patted her pockets and shrugged, hoping that was a universally understood gesture. He stepped out of view for a moment, then appeared again and handed her a signed baseball. His hand was so large that he could hide the ball in one hand, if he had to.

"I know who you are," he said suddenly in faltering English.

"Huh?"

"The girl with the blog about Rafael."

"Yes. Yes, that was me," she said. "I met him today actually," she added excitedly. "Do you know him?"

"Since we were small boys." He smiled his familiar tight-lipped smile. "He wasn't the best player, but he… tried the hardest. He never quit. He never will." His voice was full of respect.

"Nope," Maya agreed. She could tell that Hugo cared about Rafael.

"So, are you going to blog about me now?" he asked.

"No," she said. "I don't think you want me to." She walked back up the steps with her ball, leaving him to wonder what she meant.

* * *

The hard part of keeping a secret was that you had to do it every day. Maya thought of the folktale where the boy had his finger in a dike, holding off a flood. But he only had to do it one night. She had to keep the hole plugged up all day, every day.

She kept herself busy—bicycling, reading, chatting with Bijou, and listening to Kernels games. She started to learn Spanish on a free website. *El elefante es grande.* She babysat for Claire a few times and volunteered at the community garden. She saw monarch chrysalises suspended from the leaves and, on one magical afternoon, watched a butterfly tap and tear its way out of one. She sat for two hours, cross-legged on the grass, as the tiny-winged insect ventured out and sucked the dew from a leaf.

Every morning, she thought: I will not tell anyone today.

Meanwhile, Dad had a few job interviews, but nothing panned out. He found out from Mom that the community college needed a statistics professor. It was temporary, part-time work, but he applied, was interviewed, and was assigned four classes. "It'll keep body and soul together," he said.

"You'll love it," Mom said. "It's really hard, but you'll love it."

Maya read that bee populations were slowly regrouping. Their numbers were still dropping, but less rapidly than expected. "Never discount evolution," her dad said. "All animals have a way of adapting to circumstance. Even humans."

Juan Santos Garcia (or rather, Hugo) was promoted to advanced-A and started pitching for the Brevard

County Manatees in Florida. Rafael Rosales continued to play well for the Kernels, but it looked like he would stay there through the end of the season—partly because the Kernels were headed for the Midwestern League playoffs and wanted Rafael in the lineup. Maya studied the list of team affiliates for the Twins and Brewers. Rafael and Hugo might see each other in advanced-A and again in double A. The triple A teams did not play in the same league, but the Twins played the Brewers six or seven games every year. Maybe one day they would face each other in the World Series. She could only hope.

Grace had given her the ball from spring training, signed by Rafael. Now it sat on Maya's dresser next to the one signed by Hugo. The second signature was a scrawl, and she wasn't sure if Hugo had written Juan's name or forgotten himself and written his real name.

She started to plan next year's garden. She saved her babysitting money for seeds and supplies. She converted an old diaper pail of Claire's into a compost bin and scraped her family's plates into it every night. This year's garbage could be next year's soil.

If Rafael Rosales made it to Minnesota, and if he remembered their deal, she would be ready.

ACKNOWLEDGMENTS

It is audacious to write outside one's own cultural experience, but this story got hold of my imagination and did not let go. I sought information about the Dominican Republic from more sources than I can list here, but the most important are the documentary *Pelotero* made by Casey Beck and a series of articles she coauthored with Trevor Martin for the *Global Post*, the PBS Documentary *The New Americans*, the book *The Eastern Stars* by Mark Kurlansky, and *The Tropic of Baseball* by Rob L. Ruck. To better understand the land, I made use of YouTube videos, especially an hour-long tour of the streets of San Pedro de Macorís made by Guillermo Garcia de la Cruz. For descriptions of day-to-day life, I relied on numerous blogs written by people who live or traveled there. I enjoyed a delicious plate of *la bandera* and stories of the DR at the home of Seth and Tiffany Lewis. I learned much of Dominican history and culture from the marvelous books of Julia Alvarez and Junot Díaz. My playlist while writing the first draft was Proyecto Uno and Los Ilegales.

For the details about Maya's bee garden (and my own), I used resources at the University of Minnesota Extension. Dr. Jenkins is based on Dr. Marla Spivak and her work with the Minnesota Bee Lab. Anne Ursu's wonderful (but defunct) *Bat-Girl* blog inspired Grace's *Thinking Girl* blog. Sixth-graders at Olson Middle School helped me brainstorm Maya's life inside and outside of school. My wife helped me imagine Maya's room, and I borrowed the "see the rabbits" story from her family history.

I am honored to have had the support of an Artist's Initiative Grant from the Minnesota State Arts Board, which gave me both the time and the jolt of confidence I needed to see this through.

I am especially grateful to my early readers with connections to the Dominican Republic who read for accuracy and sensitivity: Dennis Hidalgo, Lidia Valdez, Angela Padron, and Betsaida Alcantara. Other important early readers include Christina Diaz Gonzalez,

Steve Brezenoff, Kelly Barnhill, Christopher Lincoln, Bryan Bliss, Jodi Chromey, Karlyn Coleman, and her son, Auggie.

People I cannot thank enough include Tina Wexler for being my coach, critic, and champion for over ten years, and Wendy McClure for giving this book a chance. Thanks to Wendy, Alex Messina-Schultheis, Kristin Zelazko, Ellen Kokontis, and everyone else at Albert Whitman & Company for seeing this book through its many stages.

Belated and eternal thanks to the many teachers, librarians, booksellers, and other book lovers who put my books—or any books—into the hands of young readers.

To my wife, Angela, and my son, Byron—I am blessed to live in a home where love is expressed as freely and frequently as it is in ours. To the rest of my friends, family, colleagues, readers, and fellow writers—you are too many to list. If you are reading this page in the hopes of seeing your name, please know that I value your friendship and hope to see you soon.